The House Children

A novel

HEIDI DANIELE

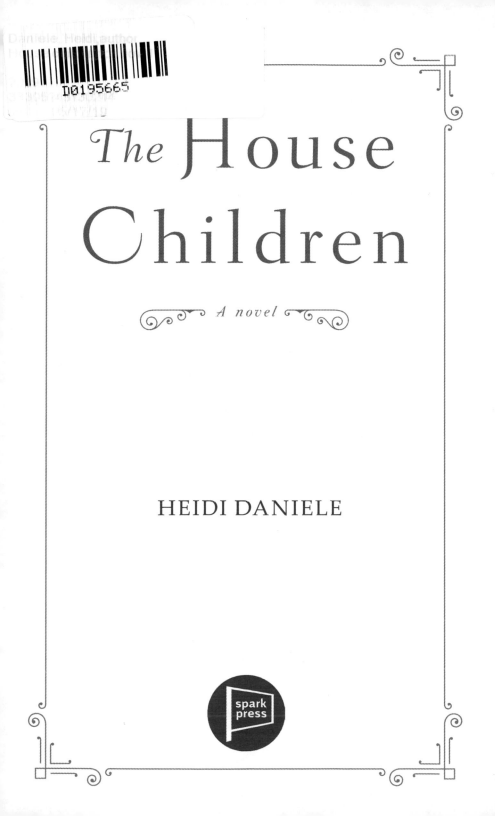

spark press

Published by SparkPress, a BookSparks imprint,
A division of SparkPoint Studio, LLC
Phoenix, Arizona, USA, 85007
www.gosparkpress.com

Published 2019
Printed in the United States of America
ISBN: 978-1-943006-94-6 (pbk)
ISBN: 978-1-943006-95-3 (e-bk)

Library of Congress Control Number: 2018959803

The House
Children

For the lovely ladies from Saint Joseph's Industrial School

"Stone on stone,
No mortar, still strong.
Like the rock walls of Ireland may you withstand the weather."

—Heidi Daniele
A Sentimental Journey

CHAPTER ONE

My birth was a sin and a crime. I was born in the Tuam Mother Baby Home to an inmate serving a year of penal servitude, her crime an out-of-wedlock pregnancy. When she was discharged, she was forced to leave me behind in the care of the Bon Secur nuns. This archaic system imposed an unbearable weight of shame that both my mother and I carried into our futures.

I'm grateful that, as I look back in time, the further I go, the fewer memories I have, but then I wonder why these particular memories have remained. I spent my first four years in that home and the only knowledge I have about it is what I've since read in newspapers. There were reports of neglect and early deaths of so many children, their bodies disposed of in a rotting septic tank in the rear of the property. So I was one of the fortunate ones with no memory of that time and having survived.

My earliest recollections are from when I lived with the Clearys, my foster family. Their small thatched cottage was in a remote town in Galway called Lissawullen. The Clearys appeared to be a typical Irish family. Mrs. Cleary ran the household, her two children went to school, and her husband was a farmer. Their home was sparsely furnished and decorated with a few Catholic pictures and statues. At first I thought they were my family, but when I called Mrs. Cleary "Mam," she quickly retorted, "I'm not yer mam, yer an illegitimate."

Mrs. Cleary's two children attended school, but she kept me home even though I was of age. When I asked if I could go to school she said, "Yer too wee ta make the long walk." Instead, rain or shine she'd send me outside where I'd wander freely around the fields and play with Sheppard, the family dog.

The sight of Mr. Cleary herding his sheep into the barn at dusk was my signal to return to the house, where I was confined to a short, three-legged stool by the hearth. At bedtime Mrs. Cleary would toss me a blanket and I'd lie down by the fireplace with Sheppard at my side. The warmth of the fire could never suppress the dampness that came up through the thin cement floor.

Each morning I'd sit quietly on my stool and watch Mrs. Cleary feed her children, and then comb their hair before they left the house. Meghan would smile and say goodbye to me as she gently pat Sheppard on the head and Sean would lean down and pinch me before walking out the front door. The first time he did it I cried and Mrs. Cleary hit me on the head, so after that I just braced myself each morning and held back my tears. After they'd leave, Sheppard would nuzzle up against my legs and we'd wait for Mrs. Cleary to feed us the leftover scraps before opening the door to let us out for the day.

The most vivid memory I have from that time happened on a summer night in 1943. Images of that night still creep into my mind and keep me from sleeping. I was sitting on my stool looking at the flames still alive in the fireplace where Mrs. Cleary had cooked supper. The air in the kitchen was hot and arid, adding to the tension that was suffocating the room. From the corner of my eye I could see Mrs. Cleary standing by the sink wiping her brow with a dishrag. Sean and Meghan were at the table eating their supper and they began to giggle and that irritated Mrs. Cleary. "You two get in the back room!"

I held my breath and watched them leave the kitchen. Mrs. Cleary went to the table and grabbed a piece of uneaten meat from one of the plates and tossed it my way. I picked it up off the floor and ate it, chewing it slowly to make it last.

The front door swung open and I looked down toward the floor and watched the dirt fall from Mr. Cleary's boots as he stumbled over to the table. "Where's my supper?"

Mrs. Cleary banged the dishes in response and then her sturdy black shoes moved across the floor toward the sink and then back to the table where I heard her set down a plate. I poked at a hole in my shirt and listened as he mocked her.

"I wouldn't feed this slop ta an animal!" he yelled and then he called for his children to come and sit with him. I heard Sean open the door and step into the kitchen. I looked up when Mrs. Cleary shouted at him, "Get back inta that room!" He quickly disappeared closing the door behind him. Then Mr. Cleary stood up and I thought he might be coming for me, but instead he shoved his wife violently and she grabbed the edge of the table to keep from falling. I looked down at the hole in my shirt, hoping he wouldn't notice me.

Suddenly Mrs. Cleary grabbed the stool out from under me and I fell backwards, my head crashing on the floor. I let out a loud cry and watched as Mr. Cleary tried to grab the stool from her as she waved it in the air before smashing it over his head. He dropped straight to the floor and lay there motionless. She stood there her face flushed, and her breath heavy, the stool still in her hand hanging at her side. I sat up and began to retch at the sight of blood pooling around Mr. Cleary's head.

"Shut up and stop yer sobbing!"

I tried to swallow my tears and slid backwards, terrified she was going to hit me next. I pulled my knees close to my chest and watched the red stream from Mr. Cleary's head slowly flow toward my shoes.

Sean came into the kitchen and stood there speechless, his

mouth agape, and Meghan began to cry and scream, "Mam, what'd ya do? What'd ya do?"

Mrs. Cleary's eyes darted from her husband, to her children, and then toward me. My eyes went back and forth between the stool in her hand and the expression on her bright, red face.

"Sean, take Meghan outside."

Sean pointed to me and asked, "What about her?"

"Leave her."

They left the house and I remained sitting on the kitchen floor shivering with fear. Mrs. Cleary stepped over her husband and tossed the stool into the fireplace. She washed her hands and then picked up her dishrag from the floor and hung it on a hook. It seemed like a long time that she stood there by the sink looking into the fire watching the stool burn. Mr. Cleary lay on the floor in a pool of blood and for a moment I thought I saw his hand move. Mrs. Cleary came toward me and I raised my hands to cover my head and she grabbed my arm, yanked me up off the floor and pulled me behind her as she walked out the front door.

"Let's go," she said to her children, swiftly moving toward the barn, dragging me behind her. When she let go of me I ran over and stood next to Meghan. Sean helped his mother open the two large doors, and Meghan and I followed them inside, silently watching as they hitched a cart to their horse, Ginger.

"Get in," Mrs. Cleary ordered Meghan. Sheppard jumped into the cart behind her and Mrs. Cleary grabbed him by the collar and yanked him off. "That dog has the mange, we ain't taking him."

I stood there waiting for my instructions.

Mrs. Cleary got into the cart and threw one of Ginger's blankets at me. "You stay put."

Sean took the reins and guided Ginger through the large opening. Once they were outside Mrs. Cleary jumped off the cart and shut the barn doors, leaving me and Sheppard behind.

It wasn't the first time I'd been left in the barn; she put me in here often, but it still scared me. I curled up on the blanket and cried. Sheppard came over and lay down beside me. Sheppard and I were the same, both of us targets of the Clearys' rage. I tried to block out the image of the pool of blood around Mr. Cleary's head streaming out across the kitchen floor.

I woke to Sheppard's wild barking and began to cry again. A woman's voice called from outside the barn. "Mary Margaret, Mary Margaret!"

One of the barn doors opened and a ray of sunlight followed a woman as she came inside. She was familiar to me, a rare visitor who'd been especially kind to me whenever she was here. She rushed over, knelt down, and wrapped her arms around me. Her embrace was comforting and she gently rocked me while I wept. "I'm so sorry, Mary Margaret, I'm so sorry," she said, and then she began to cry, too.

My memory of what happened next is vague. I recall she took me to another farm where she lived with her mother, father, and a sister.

The sisters said little amongst themselves as they washed me outside by the well and then brought me inside to feed me. I remember thinking they were so kind and gentle, and I felt safe. They didn't ask me any questions and I didn't say much. "She's still in shock," said their mother. I don't recall actually meeting their father.

I know I slept through the night in a back room on a real bed and woke up confused, unsure of where I was. The sound of people arguing lured me out of bed and I slowly cracked open the door. The family was sitting at the table, the man's back to me. He banged his fist down and said, "I want her out of here." The mother nodded her head and said, "I'll talk to Father Cosgrove." One of the sisters started to cry and the other one stood up. "But she's yer blood!" I closed the door when I heard the word "blood."

I lay back down on the bed and cried thinking about the Clearys and that I didn't want to go back there. The older lady came into the bedroom and patted me on the head. "Now yer ta ferget what ya saw over there," she said and wiped my face dry. Then she asked me, "Are ya hungry?" and I nodded my head and forced a smile.

The older lady left the house and the sisters fed me, dressed me and then took me outside. They told me to stay by the house and to keep out of the fields. I knew it had something to do with the man cutting turf in the distance. I sensed they were trying to keep me out of his sight and I was familiar with that feeling.

The following morning the sisters fussed over me, washing me, brushing my hair until it was smooth, and dressing me in a pretty blue frock. I enjoyed the attention and recall thinking about how lovely it would be to stay with them. My fondest memory of that morning was when the woman that found me in the barn scooped me up into her arms and her sister said, "Smile fer the camera." That was the first and only time I had my picture taken as a child.

The sisters laughed and played with me outside while their mother sat somberly on a chair by the front door. Their mood changed quickly when a black car pulled up in front of the house and a lady dressed in a dark skirt and white blouse emerged from the passenger seat.

The next thing I remember is feeling a hand on my back gently pushing me toward the car and someone saying, "Go on now, Mary Margaret. Mrs. Moran will see ta it that yer taken care of."

"Am I goin back ta the Cleary's?" I asked Mrs. Moran as she helped me into the back seat. She smiled and said, "No."

It was a relief to hear that, but I was still scared of the unknown ahead of me. I stood up on the seat and looked out the rear window as the car pulled away from the curb. I waved to the three women. One of them waved back, the older lady looked down, and the other one brought her hands up to cover her face.

We drove for what seemed like a long time, down narrow country roads and through small villages, before coming into the small town of Ballinasloe. The driver stopped in front of the district court house, a large, intimidating gray building.

"Pick me up at the convent in about two hours," Mrs. Moran said to the driver and then she led me into the building.

We entered a noisy crowded courtroom. The judge, robed in black, sat in front at a high table, his clerk beside him. I sat down next to an impish-looking boy close to my age. Mrs. Moran handed me a biscuit and then sorted some papers she'd removed from her satchel. The boy next to me eyed my treat and I could tell he was hungry, so I slid it over to him.

Silence took over the room when the clerk stood up. "Malcolm O'Neill, ten years old, charged with missin school fer two months and not havin a parent that'll exercise proper guardianship."

All eyes followed the garda and the young boy he escorted down the aisle. After looking over some papers the judge said, "Sentenced ta four years in the Certified Industrial School Artane, ta be cared fer by the Christian Brothers in Dublin."

The room filled with whispers about Artane, and a woman behind me began to cry. The judge slammed down his gavel. The noise caused me to jump and the room was silent again.

One child after another was brought before the judge and sentenced to one industrial school or another.

My heart dropped to the pit of my stomach when the clerk called, "Mary Margaret Joyce, six years old, the charge is destitute and not an orphan."

Mrs. Moran tugged at me to get up and follow her, and I held back the tears as everyone looked at me walking down the aisle. The judge reviewed the papers and then asked, "Parent consent?"

Mrs. Moran quickly replied, "Yes yer honor. The mother is unable ta support her. The child is illegitimate."

The judge lifted his spectacles and looked down at me. "Mary Margaret Joyce, sentenced ta nine years in the Certified Industrial School Saint Thomas, ta be cared fer by the Sisters of Mercy in Ballinasloe."

CHAPTER TWO

The afternoon air was warm when we left the courthouse and I wanted to run, but I had nowhere to go. Instead, I walked with Mrs. Moran down Society Street to Saint Thomas' Convent. She pushed open the heavy iron gate that led to an ornate door and rang the bell. A teenage girl with big brown eyes, auburn hair, and a bright smile welcomed us into a grand foyer. After a brief exchange, Bridget, the girl with the sunny personality, picked up a striker and hit a gong-like bell, sending reverberations up a wide staircase and down the hallways.

A few moments later, my eyes were drawn upward to the large woman with a broad, steely face descending the stairs. She was dressed in black from head to toe, and a clinking sound came from the wooden beads and leather strap that swung from her waist with every step she took.

"Good day, Sister Constance," said Mrs. Moran. Then she motioned toward me. "This is the admission Father Cosgrove sent."

Sister Constance looked me over with a critical eye, making me feel like an object instead of a person. Her presence overwhelmed me, and I watched her large hand as it reached for the papers Mrs. Moran brought from the courthouse. She told Bridget to serve us tea in Saint

Andrew's Parlor and then left the foyer. I sighed with relief when she disappeared down one of the mysterious corridors.

Bridget beckoned us into an elegant room, where Mrs. Moran settled herself into one of the four brocade-covered chairs around a highly polished table. I felt daunted by the opulent surroundings but my attention was quickly diverted when Bridget returned carrying a silver tray laden with baked goods and a pot of tea. Bridget smiled at me and said, "Now don't ya worry, sure it's the Mercys that've reared me, and I'm just fine!"

The scones were delicious and I helped myself to a second one, slathering it with butter and jam. Sister Constance reappeared just as I was licking the excess off my fingers. I jumped off the chair and put my hand behind my back as if to hide evidence of my guilt. She gave me a glaring look and then handed Mrs. Moran an envelope.

"We'd appreciate anything you can do to bring us up to capacity. We've room for eleven more."

Mrs. Moran left the room and Sister Xavier came in with a ledger.

"I have recorded Mary Margaret's information and assigned her number 27."

Sister Constance glanced at the documents.

"Change her name to Peg, we have too many Marys."

Then she instructed me to take a seat on the bench just outside the parlor door. Biting down on my lower lip, trying not to cry, I wiped away the random tear that escaped.

A woman with short cropped hair and slightly hunched shoulders shuffled over to me.

"Isn't that a pretty blue frock ya got on?"

I forced a smile and looked up at her, surprised to see how young she was.

"I'm Katie Robbins, and I'm ta see ya get settled in."

"I'm Mary Margaret."

"Not in here, dear. From now on, yer Peg or number 27."

She extended her dry, calloused hand, with fingernails bitten to the quick, and took me down a hallway. I pulled from her grip as we left the convent through a rear door. A path led us to a garden adjacent to a large gray building. Standing at the edge of the garden I looked toward two nuns strolling through the flower beds.

"Yer never ta go inta the garden," said Katie. "Tis where the nuns go ta walk and pray."

Then she turned toward the building and I followed her up the wide stone steps to a white door. As she reached for the knob, a voice rose from the far side of the stoop.

"Hello Katie, who've you got with you today?"

Katie pushed me toward the voice. "Hello, Sister Carmel, this is Peg."

The nun stood up and put her spade on the step. Her round jovial face, encased in black, beamed a bright red.

"Welcome Peg, welcome to Saint Thomas', may God bless you."

❀

We entered a plain room with bare windows and a few old chairs strewn on a tattered rug.

"This is Saint Luke's Parlor, where ya'll have yer visitors."

Passing through a glass-paned door we stopped at the base of a wide staircase.

"Yer never ta go up these stairs. They're fer Sister Constance."

We continued down the hall and Katie showed me the girls' toilet room with two stalls.

"This is it fer all the girls, so no dilly dallying in here."

She didn't seem to notice Sister Constance scolding a girl in the next room. She just pointed and said, "That's the rec room where we say the nightly rosary."

I nodded, even though I had no idea what a nightly rosary was.

A blast of intense heat hit me in the face when we entered the laundry, where two women immediately looked up from their pedal-driven sewing machines. Several girls behind them didn't appear to notice us; they continued working, poking long sticks in large tubs, pushing garments through rollers, and ironing mountains of clothes.

One of the women stood up and rested her hands on her wide hips.

"I'm Julia Cassidy, head seamstress here, and what're we callin ya?"

"I'm Mary Mar . . ."

Katie tugged the back of my dress. "Call her Peg, she's number 27."

"I'm Peg," I said.

Tears welled up in my eyes as I felt forced to abandon the one thing that was mine. Julia reached over and patted me on the shoulder.

"Ah, it takes a bit of time ta get used ta, lass. Don't ya worry."

A pretty, green-eyed girl with long red hair walked toward us, carrying a basket of wet clothes.

She winked at me and said, "Hi ya, cutie pie!" and then she barked at Katie, "Move yer arse outa my way!"

Katie scrunched her face and lurched into a side-step as the girl barreled past her.

"That Angela O'Neill is such a cheeky one," Katie said.

Julia nodded, "Too big fer her britches, she is. Now Peg, let me see yer feet."

I lifted my right foot, then my left.

Julia looked at my feet and then scanned me from head to toe, calculating my measurements.

"I'll have ta check the boot room. I'll have Peg's things ready after supper."

We left the laundry and went toward a door that had been left slightly ajar. As we got closer, the sound of voices increased and we stepped out into a yard crowded with young girls, all wearing the same gray farm clothes.

"I want ya ta stick with the wee ones yer own age," said Katie.

She grabbed a lanky girl with dark hair and milky white skin. "This is Mary. She'll show ya around."

"I don't know what she wants me ta show ya. This is the yard. The only way out is through the gate at the back wall, and that's locked."

Mary introduced me to a few of the girls and I became self-conscious of the frock I was wearing. It was intimidating to be in the midst of so many other children. I was glad when Katie returned, ringing a hand bell to call the girls in for supper. I queued up and followed them into the refectory, a dull beige room with windows overlooking the nuns' garden. I sat next to Mary on one of the benches at three long communal tables set with tarnished tin mugs and plates.

The appearance of Sister Constance in the doorway extinguished the chatter in the room and the girls folded their hands and bowed their heads. I did the same. Their voices melded together and in unison they prayed.

"Bless us oh Lord, and these Thy gifts which we are about to receive from Thy bounty, through Christ our Lord. Amen."

I wasn't familiar with the words but it sounded lovely and I wanted to be a part of their chorus.

Sister Constance left the room and the girls began to converse in whispers. Four older girls poured cocoa into our mugs and set out platters of bread that were quickly emptied as each girl grabbed her share. The cocoa tasted watery and the spread on the bread was greasy, but it was filling.

In the evening, Mary showed me the cubbies along the back wall in the rec room, one for each girl to store her special items. She was about to show me the contents of hers when the overhead light flashed, and the girls dropped to their knees and folded their hands again. While they prayed, I thought about the nice ladies I'd stayed with, and wished I were still with them. My knees began to hurt and I wanted to stand up, but the watchful eye of Sister Constance told me it wouldn't be a wise move.

At bedtime, we filed up a narrow staircase to the second floor and the girls dispersed into two dorm rooms, each furnished with fifty metal beds lined up in three rows. Katie escorted me to dorm two, row three, bed fourteen, where a short stack of gray farm clothes sat neatly folded, each piece marked with the number 27. She gave me a pair of shoes with metal bits hammered into the sole and told me to store my things in the box below the bed.

Along with the other girls, I stripped off my clothes and put on a nightdress and lined up to use the washroom. We washed up without any soap and shared the few small towels. Sister Agnes, a small scrawny nun, monitored the washroom to ensure we weren't fooling around or drinking water from the tap.

"Some of the girls say Sister Agnes is the meanest one of em all," Mary informed me.

When I returned to the dorm, my blue dress and shoes were gone. I would have liked to have kept the dress, but at least with these other clothes I wouldn't stand out. The overhead light flashed, and the girls dropped to their knees and folded their hands, and the chorus began.

"Now I lay me down ta sleep, I pray the Lord my soul ta keep. If I shall die before I wake, I pray the Lord my soul ta take. Amen."

I was thankful it was a short one.

The metal bars beneath the thin mattress dug into my side and it took a few twists and turns before I settled into a comfortable spot. I looked out through the bare window at the new moon, and listened to the beds creak, the low whispers and soft cries. I turned my face to the thin pillow and allowed my own tears to emerge. This didn't seem like a terrible place, but I just didn't understand. Why was I here?

The next morning, the loud clanging of a bell woke me. I looked up. It was Sister Constance. Everyone jumped out of their beds and began folding their linens. An older girl came over to help me.

The light flickered and we were praying again.

"Father in heaven, ya love me. Yer with me night n day. I want ya ta love me always. In all I do and say, I'll try ta please ya. Father, bless me through the day. Amen."

Afterwards, we stood at attention beside our beds as Sister Constance walked down the aisles, inspecting our linens. She pulled the sheet off one girl's bed and threw it at her. The girl took the sheet and walked over to the doorway. The same thing happened to three others, and when Sister Constance left the room, they followed her. The girl next to me whispered, "Bedwetters."

That morning I experienced a pleasant sense of belonging. Dressed in my gray farm clothes, I queued up to go to the convent chapel, where we filed into pews behind several rows of nuns. The curtain of black cloth in front of me obstructed my view of the one-man show. Unfamiliar with the ceremony and rituals, I followed the movements of the others, standing, sitting, and kneeling. When I went to join the line for communion, Mary pulled me down into my seat.

"Not yet, we aren't ready."

Over a breakfast of cocoa and lumpy porridge, Mary told me that we'd be prepared for First Holy Communion in Primary School and that would start in three weeks. I liked having something to look forward to.

The next hour was scheduled for daily chores. I was assigned to polish the floor moldings on the second floor with Ellen, a plump girl with frizzy red hair. While we worked, Ellen told me her mam went mad and was put into an asylum after her pa died. She said Sister Constance changed her age so she'd be old enough to stay here with her sisters, otherwise she'd be in foster care. I began to tell her about the Clearys, and Ellen held up her hand to silence me.

"Listen, here she comes."

Sure enough, I heard the sound of the wooden beads and leather strap clinking as she climbed the steps. We stood up together and greeted her, "Good Morning, Sister Constance."

She nodded and continued down the hallway.

Once she was out of sight, Ellen told me Sister Constance sleeps in one of the cells just past our dorm and the other nuns take turns sleeping in the second cell.

Back down on my knees, I dipped my rag in the tin of polish and rubbed it into the molding. My thoughts of Sister Constance were beginning to soften. I slid backwards and polished a bit more, glancing over at Ellen as she worked on the other side; I wondered if maybe my mam was in an asylum, too.

❧

During the next two weeks I embraced the comfort of routine and a sense of belonging. I enjoyed my new friends and felt their concern for me. Ellen fed me general tips: try to get the last pour of cocoa because the mix settles at the bottom of the pitcher, and tell Julia you need the next size up, because the looser the clothing, the less it scratches your skin. Mary was more focused on the rules. She told me the dos and don'ts of Saint Thomas' Industrial School, and there were many. I tried to follow her simple solution: "Stay out of Sister Constance's view!"

There were some things about the industrial school that I didn't like. For example, there was absolutely nowhere to go to be alone, except in one of the two toilet stalls. And although I was grateful for my meals, Sister Virginia was a terrible cook and she fed us the same thing every day. The one thing I really hated was being confined within the high stone walls of the yard. But on the whole, living here was good, and it was certainly better than at the Clearys'.

Close to a hundred girls resided in Saint Thomas' Industrial School, and half as many nuns lived in the convent. I learned there were two types of nuns: the educated choir nuns, and the lay nuns. Sister Constance was a choir nun, trained as a nurse, and our House Manager. Some girls said the Devil himself would fear her. She was strict and sometimes cruel, but she treated all the girls the same way— she had no pets. I'd heard some nuns had pets, and all of the girls longed to become one, because then you'd get a little extra attention.

At the start of my third week, Primary School opened and I was enrolled in First Class. After our morning jobs, we assembled in the yard and Katie unlocked the gate and sent us up the lane. We crossed a grass lawn and entered the Primary School through the back door. Our classroom had four rows of desks, each one large enough to accommodate two students. I took the empty seat in the third row, next to a girl wearing a yellow frock. Her golden hair was tied up in a bow, and her hazel eyes twinkled when she said hello to me.

Our teacher was a tall, skinny nun with severe facial features. She stood at her desk, straight as a pin, holding a ruler in her right hand, and tapping it in the palm of her left.

Sister Frances spoke slowly and deliberately as she outlined her expectations. Our first lesson was about the Sacrament of Penance. She said her intention was to bring us to the path of God's forgiveness and keep us out of hell, an evil place where the Devil lived in the midst of burning flames.

During the lesson I glanced behind me and noticed Ellen had fallen asleep. Sister Frances' face reddened with anger as she noticed, too. A grim silence took over the room, and I sat as still as a corpse as Sister Frances walked down the aisle past me. All eyes were riveted on her ruler as she poked Ellen. The color drained from her chubby face when she looked up.

"Hands on the desk, palm side down," Sister Frances demanded.

I held my breath watching her raise the ruler high in the air, and

I clenched my fists when she whipped it down, fast and hard, onto Ellen's knuckles.

WHACK!

Ellen shrieked in pain, and Sister Frances hit her again and again.

The girl next to me closed her eyes and covered her ears with her hands, I slid my fists beneath my thighs. Sister Frances returned to her desk and continued with the lesson and I kept my eyes wide open while listening to Ellen weeping behind me.

At noon, an announcement came through a loudspeaker in the corner of the room.

"House children stand. House children go."

I sat and watched the girls in the row behind me rise up from their seats and line up by the door. The girl in the yellow dress nudged me.

"That's fer you, too."

It was at that moment I realized it was only the girls in gray farm clothes that were lined up. I felt the class watching me as I walked over to join them. Sister Frances opened the door and we filed into the hallway already filled with girls from the industrial school exiting through the rear door.

Mary ran over to me as I walked down the lane.

"Why didn't ya get up?"

I shrugged my shoulders.

"We are the house children! And we're not allowed ta get friendly with the town children, so don't be chattin it up with the girl in the yellow frock."

I felt bad for Ellen. She sat alone while we ate our midday meal and refused to walk with us when we returned to class. It was only our first day and Sister Frances had already put the fear of God in me. I vowed to do whatever was necessary to stay in her good graces and keep out of hell.

As we headed back to class, Angela walked by us with a basket of wet clothes. She smiled and said hello.

"Where's she goin?"

"Ta hang laundry on the lines down by the river."

"Why doesn't she go ta school?"

"Not all the girls go ta school," said Mary. "If yer not good at learnin or the nuns don't like ya, they'll keep ya back fer cleanin."

The following days were more of the same. Sister Frances read aloud and we repeated everything she said verbatim. Her class was boring and predictable, but there was comfort in the routine and I preferred to be in the classroom than confined in the yard. I also enjoyed the occasional moment when I was able to talk with Catherine, the girl who sat next to me. She told me her dad had a small orchard on the other side of the wall in our yard, and I was delighted when she invited me to play after school.

"My mam said we're all God's children and I can be yer friend."

I broached the topic with Mary and she advised me to squelch the idea. I knew she was right—the nuns wouldn't let me go over to her house.

At the end of September, news spread about the arrival of Sister Angela, a young, energetic nun who had recently entered the convent. Sister Constance arranged for her to give us singing lessons on Tuesdays in the rec room after class. Everyone loved her. She glided around the room like she was floating on air and she always had a smile on her face. Her skin was fair and smooth, and wavy strands of auburn hair slipped out from under her veil. She defied all the things I'd come to believe about nuns. I wanted to touch her to see if she was real, and when she slipped me a sweet one day, I tried to hold onto her hand. Sometimes at night, I dreamt I was her pet, and Tuesday became my favorite day of the week.

The weekdays weren't bad but I hated the weekends, and Friday nights were the worst. We trudged our dirty clothes and linens down to the large bins and then lined up for a bath in one of three deep tubs in the back of the laundry. One after another we'd take a turn dipping ourselves in soapy water for two or three minutes to wash up. It was awful, and if you were toward the end of the line, the water would be cold and dirty. Wrapped up in tiny towels, we'd run to the rec room and wait for our number to be called to collect a clean set of clothes and linens. There were many fights over the few combs available, as we tried to keep our hair from drying up in knots.

Saturdays we'd sit in the yard, waiting to see who'd appear at the gate. Ellen's grandmother usually showed up and she'd pass sweets to her, which Ellen quickly gobbled up. The local boys could be counted on to come and cause a ruckus. Once they were throwing dead frogs at us and one hit Mary. She was so mad that she started yelling and cussing at them. I thought Sister Constance was coming to Mary's defense when she rushed into the yard with her long stick, but instead she started hitting Mary with it. I hated watching anyone get hit, especially one of my friends.

If the weather was fair on a Sunday, Katie took us for a walk to the train station and back. I'd try to pair up with Bridget for the walks because she made up little rhymes and quips that kept me laughing. One thing that was different about Bridget was that she never spoke poorly of the nuns. She said she'd always be grateful to them for taking her in.

∞

Ballinasloe held a week-long horse fair every October on the green across the street from the Primary School. Looking out at the fairgrounds from the classroom window was like torture for me. Fortunately, Tofts Amusements, the vendor for the large mechanical rides, gave free passes to the house children on the last day of the fair. I'll never forget the first time I went.

I was bursting with anticipation as Katie handed out the passes on Saturday morning. Before unlocking the gate, she made an announcement warning us to keep away from the tinkers.

"They've got bad blood in em, and they're known fer stealing little girls."

With my pass clenched in my fist, I linked arms with Mary and ran up the lane and across Society Street. I was immediately drawn to a cluster of brightly painted wagons, where a group of people, dressed in colorful clothes, sat on wooden crates. They clapped their hands to the beat of the lively music that played and watched their children dance.

"Tinkers," Mary whispered in my ear.

They appeared to be a happy clan, and I thought to myself that it wouldn't be such a terrible thing to be stolen by them.

Mary pulled me over to the games and rides, where we lined up for the Big Dipper. I thought I might get sick when our bucket stopped and lingered for a few moments at the very top. Mary took the opportunity to point out the River Suck behind the industrial school, and then she suggested the perfect crime for us to commit in preparation for our first confession.

"My sister Theresa and her friends are goin foxin over ta the nuns' orchard, let's go with them."

I needed a sin to confess, so I quickly agreed. We found Theresa and joined her group running down the lane, past the gate, past the clothes lines and into the nuns' orchard by the river. Some of the girls climbed up the trees, while others jumped up to grab apples from the branches. Mary and I sat by the river stuffing ourselves with golden, juicy apples, feeling proud to have a sin under our belt.

It poured on the day we made our first confession, and with our hands over our heads we ran down the street and turned into Saint Michael's Square. We rushed toward Saint Michael's Church, with its spire rising so high it appeared to pierce the clouds. I was so worried about what I was going to say in the confessional that I didn't pay any attention to the town itself. We entered the church soaking wet to find a very dry Sister Frances waiting for us.

She lined us up by height, putting me at the front of the line, and then ushered us halfway down the aisle and into a pew. I sat down and looked in awe at my surroundings. The ornate ceiling was at least three stories high and the walls were graced with paintings of the Stations of the Cross, each one separated by an enormous stained-glass window. Sister Frances told us the church was God's house, so I'd expected it to be majestic. I wondered if God was here right now. Interrupting my thoughts, she tapped me on the shoulder and pointed to the confessional.

I pushed the heavy red velvet curtain to the side and stepped into the small cubicle. I knelt down on the red leather kneeler and rested my folded hands on the shelf beneath a small window. The window slid open and a screen separated me from the priest. I whispered my confession to him, and he told me to say two Hail Marys and three Our Fathers for penance and then I recited my act of contrition. When it was over I returned to the pew feeling very relieved.

The rain had stopped by the time we were done and Katie tried to urge us along, but we took our time. At Phalen's Sweet Shoppe we pressed our faces against the window to ogle the goods on display, and then we made a game of guessing what was in the oven as we passed the bakery. We stopped to admire the haberdashery window until the sales clerk came out and shooed us away. I could have stayed in the square all day watching the townspeople go about their business. I thought I'd look forward to our weekly confessional trip to Saint Michael's, but that changed.

In November the weather turned raw, and we raced through town without coats or gloves to go to confession every Saturday. There was no reason good enough to linger by the shoppes in the bitter cold.

When we returned to the industrial school, we were sent back into the yard regardless of the temperature. The younger girls crowded together to keep warm while the older girls snuck into the boiler room. Many of the girls got sick, and Sister Constance prescribed a daily dose of cod liver oil to help prevent winter ailments. So each morning Katie plunged a spoonful of it into our mouths, using the same spoon for everyone. It tasted awful, the smell was horrible, and the girls still got sick. Bedwetting increased during the cold months, and sometimes up to a dozen girls would follow Sister Constance out of the room after inspection. She took them down to the laundry and dunked them into an ice bath, believing that would remedy their problem. Thankfully, I never wet the bed, but I did have one terrible bladder incident in class.

I raised my hand and asked if I could use the toilet; Sister Frances said no. When I raised my hand a second time, she just shook her head no. I wanted to cry because I didn't know why she kept refusing me and I felt like my bladder was going to bust open. I tried to hold it in, but I couldn't, and I peed in my seat. Catherine saw what happened and I hoped she wouldn't say anything. I knew Sister Frances would be furious and everyone would make fun of me. I looked at the clock. It was almost noon. I tried to think of a way to leave without anyone noticing.

"House children stand. House children go."

I stayed seated until the girls behind me got up and then I slowly stood, moving my hands behind me, trying to cover up the wetness. I walked toward the door with my back to the wall, hoping no one would notice.

"She peed! She peed!" said one the town's children, pointing at me.

I felt the panic build inside of me, and Sister Frances immediately got up from her desk. Her eyes were fixed on me. She grabbed me by the ear and pulled me to the front of the classroom. My ear stung with pain and I wanted to cry, but I held back the tears.

"Hands on the desk, palm side down."

I had dreaded this moment since the first day of class. Tears welled up in my eyes and I couldn't hold them back any longer as I placed my hands on her desk. Through the puddles in my eyes, I followed the ruler as she lifted it in the air and then I looked pleadingly at her normally pale face, which was now flushed with red. I felt her dark eyes piercing through me, and to this day I could swear a grin appeared on her face before I closed my eyes.

WHACK!

I shrieked, pain searing into my hand and I kept my eyes closed while the tears poured down my cheeks. I held my breath while I waited for the next one, but it never came.

"You little egit," she said. "You can reveal this bad bit in confession."

My knuckles burned and I sobbed as I left the classroom with the other house children, but in an odd way, I felt grateful she only hit me once.

The winter wasn't all bad, because the nuns loved Christmas. In December, before the first Sunday in Advent, Sister Angela would take a group of girls to the countryside to gather baskets of ivy and fragrant fir branches. She used the greens along with silver bells to transform the dreary rec room for the festive holiday. During our singing lessons, she taught us Christmas carols along with the hymns, and everyone was in a good mood despite the cold weather. On Christmas Day, Sister Virginia surprised us all with a tasty meal of potato cakes and minced meat with bits of currants and sultans.

She also made green Jell-O for dessert. Even Sister Constance was in better form. She gave each of us a brown bag containing a new pair of socks, a pencil, a pad of paper and an orange. Instead of being sent out in the yard, we were allowed to stay in the rec room where we sang and danced all afternoon.

Those first few months I felt happy and content living in Saint Thomas' Industrial School, until I heard about Bridget leaving. In January, I learned she was being sent to a town called Althone to live with a family and care for their two children. The thought of her leaving was upsetting and I worried about myself having to go, too. Bridget assured me that I'd see her again.

"I'll be back ta visit. Don't ya worry, Peg, by the time yer fifteen ya'll be ready ta go yerself."

CHAPTER THREE

We returned to class in January, and Sister Frances began to prepare us for our First Holy Communion. Her explanation about the Liturgy of the Eucharist left me confused and somewhat doubtful, but I didn't dare question her. Instead, I asked Mary what she thought.

"Doesn't matter what ya think," she said, "and stop askin silly questions and just start believin it before ya get in trouble."

If I'd only been as pragmatic as Mary, I could've saved myself a lot of grief.

In mid-May, Sister Frances made the announcement we'd all been waiting to hear.

"This Saturday you will be taking the Sacrament of First Holy Communion in Saint Michael's Church."

Along with the rest of the class, I fluttered with excitement until she told us that the house children would be making theirs separately in the convent chapel on Friday.

While the rest of the house children ate breakfast on Friday morning, nine of us were in the washroom, being scrubbed down by Julia and Katie. A rack loaded with white dresses mysteriously appeared in the hallway and when I reached up to touch one, Julia quickly slapped my hand back.

"I know what'll fit ya best."

She picked a dress with embroidered flowers along the hem, helped me slip it on, and fastened the pearl buttons down the back. Katie secured a simple tulle veil on my head and gave me a pair of short socks and white patent-leather shoes.

On our way to the chapel my stomach growled and my head felt dizzy. I turned to Ellen behind me and said, "I feel sick."

"Well, don't ya pass out," she said, "cause that'll be the end of ya if ya do!"

She was right. I'd seen many a girl get sick at mass, and then get a good lashing for disrupting the service.

Sister Constance stood at the chapel door. She looked us over, gave a nod of approval, and motioned for us to go inside. Nervously, I walked down the aisle, genuflected before the altar, and then took a seat in the first pew. As we sang the opening hymn, I watched Father Doherty bow in front of the tabernacle and kiss the altar before going to the podium.

I paid close attention to the mass waiting to see the transformation of bread and wine into the body and blood of Christ; but colored prisms shining through the stained-glass windows distracted me. I felt like God was looking down on me, and although I'd missed the miracle, my skepticism was replaced with a feeling of reverence.

After the mass, we gathered for a special breakfast in the refectory, where Sister Constance presented each of us with a religious medal and then gave us permission to go into the nuns' garden. I walked through the flower beds, admiring my shiny medal, a treasure I'd keep in my cubby to remember this day.

Our lessons at the Primary School ended in mid-June, and we traded in our shoes for summer sandals. The walls of the yard obstructed any breeze from the river, making the sunshine feel even hotter. On some days it was unbearable and a few girls would strip down to their knickers at the risk of getting a beating. It wasn't the heat that got to me as much as the boredom, and I often wished to be back in class with Sister Frances.

It was Saturday, the ninth of July, and we'd just finished saying the rosary when Sister Constance announced that she had arranged for us to take a trip to the strand on Monday. As we roared with excitement she raised her hand to silence us, and then read off a list of numbers.

"If your number was called, remain in the room. The rest of you may leave now."

She had called my number, 27, and I stood there frozen. Ellen looked at me with raised eyebrows and Mary whispered, "Start sayin yer prayers!"

Fear built up inside of me as I tried to think of what I did wrong. Fourteen girls including myself remained, and I didn't know any of them. Sister Constance handed each of us an empty brown paper bag as she began to speak.

"You will be leaving tomorrow for a one-week holiday. Katie will distribute envelopes with the details after morning mass. Summer holiday is a privilege, and I expect each of you to be at your best. If I receive any reports of bold behavior, you will be punished. You may use these bags to pack your things into."

She gave us a good long stare, then a quick smile and left the room. I followed the others upstairs with a bag tucked under my arm and listened to the girls ahead of me talking.

"No matter where we go, it has ta be better than here."

"Don't be so sure. Last summer I was sent ta Dublin ta care fer Father Doherty's widowed sister, and that was no holiday!"

"Sure, I'll be cleaning the whole week while I stay with my aunt."

"One of the girls that went on holiday last year never came back!"

Listening to their comments about going on holiday left me feeling discouraged. Going to the strand for a day with my friends was much more appealing than spending a week with people I didn't know. That night I couldn't fall asleep, wondering where I was being sent to.

In the morning after mass Katie gave out the envelopes.

"Pack yer bag after breakfast and meet up in Saint Luke's. Peg, I'll have Sheila look after ya on the train."

In my envelope was a piece of paper that read, "MRS. NORAH HANLEY," and a train ticket to Galway. During breakfast, I poked at the cold lump of gray porridge with my spoon while the other girls gabbed about going to the strand. Without warning, Mary snatched the envelope I'd tucked in my waistband and scornfully examined its contents.

"Hmmm, do ya know her?"

"I don't think so," I said.

"Well, maybe she's a relation. Have ya ever been ta Galway City?"

I shook my head no and took back the envelope.

Ellen got up from the table. "Have fun, Peg. I'll miss ya."

I forced a smile and then looked over at Mary.

"I hope we see ya again!" she said.

I stopped at my cubby to get my medal before going upstairs to pack, just in case I wasn't coming back. I carefully put it between my two sets of clothes and my sleeping gown in the paper bag.

I joined the others and we walked to the station, where five of us waited on the westbound platform, and the others, going to Dublin, waited on the eastbound side. We waved to each other across the tracks until the train came into sight, billowing smoke and blowing its whistle. Sheila, a much older girl, held my arm as we boarded the train and looked for an empty seat. I slid in first and sat on my knees to look out of the window. We rode through spans of countryside and little towns and after a while it all looked the same. When the other three girls got off in Athenry, I asked Sheila how much longer to Galway City.

"Tis the last stop," she said. "You'll know we're close when ya see the water."

It felt like we'd been traveling for nearly an hour before it came into view, and I was dazzled by the sight of the blue waves with beams of yellow sunshine bouncing off the water. Hypnotized by the vastness of the Galway Bay, I hadn't noticed that the train was slowing down until the whistle blew, and suddenly I felt sick as the train came to a screeching halt. Sheila handed me my bag, gripped me by the arm and led me out onto the crowded platform. I felt panicky looking around at all the people.

"How am I ta find Mrs. Hanley? I don't know who she is, or what she looks like!"

"I'll stay with ya till she comes," said Sheila. "Don't ya be worryin. These'll be nice people, it's not like yer gettin fostered out, they ain't gettin paid ta keep ya. Now if ya were bigger, I'd be thinkin they need ya fer cleanin or watchin the little ones, but yer just a wee bit of thing yerself."

∞

I recognized the woman waving and rushing toward us; it was the lady who found me in the Clearys' barn. She was smiling as she bent down to hug me, but I instinctively jumped back, preferring not to be touched.

"Don't mind her, Mrs. Hanley," said Sheila. "We don't get any hugs at the industrial school, so she ain't used ta that. But don't ya worry—she's well-behaved."

Sheila said she'd meet me back here next Sunday at noon and then disappeared into the crowd, and I stood there, not knowing what to do.

Mrs. Hanley reached for my bag. "I'll carry that fer ya, Mary Margaret."

"That's okay," I said, "and ya can call me Peg, that's what they call me now."

"Do ya remember me?" she asked.

I nodded yes, feeling relieved that she was familiar to me.

Galway City was nothing like the little town of Ballinasloe, so I stayed close to her side as we navigated through the bustle of people. Once we were out of the city center heading up a steep hill she began to talk, telling me she'd gotten married and no longer lived on the farm with her parents. At the top of the hill, she stopped in front of a small white house with a bright red door.

"This is where I live now," she said proudly, pointing to her house. "And ya'll be stayin here with us."

As she opened the door, the aroma of freshly baked bread jogged my memory, reminding me of the two days I'd spent with her in Moycullen. We entered into a large room. To my left was a sitting area and to the right was the kitchen, where a table covered with a yellow cloth was set for tea.

"Go on and sit down while I put on the kettle," she said.

I took a seat at the table and looked over at a large cupboard dominating the back wall. It was filled with dishes and framed photographs. Mrs. Hanley filled the kettle and placed it on an electric cooker, then she took the bread cooling on the window sill and cut it. My mouth watered as she spread generous amounts of butter and jam on several slices, and placed them onto a platter. When the kettle whistled, she poured the tea, leaving hers black, and adding milk and a few lashings of sugar to mine. As I stuffed myself and drank the sweet warm tea, she asked me questions about the industrial school. I was careful to only share the things I knew Sister Constance would approve of. When we were done eating, there was an awkward silence and I felt uncomfortable.

"Peg, I want ya ta feel at home here. I've made up a room fer ya, and we've got a yard fer ya ta play in, and I think ya'll like Dan, Mr. Hanley. He'll be home in a bit, he just went fer a chat with his pals at the pub."

She showed me the room I'd be sleeping in and then we went out to the yard, bordered with blooming rhododendrons. While she took the laundry off the line, I peered through the bushes at the children playing in the neighboring yard.

Later, while Mrs. Hanley prepared supper, I sat in one of the green chairs flanking the fireplace, thumbing through a book she'd given me. I was more interested in what she was doing and watched her fill a black pot with meat and vegetables which she hung on a hook in the fireplace.

"That'll take a while ta cook," she said. "Why don't we go fer a walk?"

I was glad to be outside and welcomed our stroll between the rows of tombstones in the cemetery. Together we read some of the epitaphs and admired the carvings on the stones, and gradually the awkwardness between us lessened. By the time we returned to the house I felt a bit more comfortable and quite hungry.

I was helping Mrs. Hanley set the table when the front door swung open and a tall, broad-shouldered man came into the house. In one sweeping move he removed his tweed cap, revealing a mostly bald head. He hung the cap on a hook by the door and slid across the room. Before I knew it, he was down on one knee in front of me and we were face to face, his blue eyes twinkling like the Galway Bay.

"Would ya be Mary Margaret?" he asked.

"Dan, call her Peg," said Mrs. Hanley.

I couldn't help but smile at him.

"Okay, Peg it is then. Well Peg, I've got one question fer ya," he said in a serious voice.

I straightened my back and for a moment I thought I'd done something wrong.

Then he asked me, "How are the nuns treatin ya?"

I hesitated for a second, recalling Sister Constance's warning.

"They're very nice, especially Sister Constance," I replied.

"I don't believe ya!" he said, and then he roared out laughing.

I couldn't help myself and started to giggle.

During supper Mr. Hanley entertained us with stories he'd heard at the pub and Mrs. Hanley gave me a second serving. Later in the evening, she ran a bath for me and allowed me to soak in the tub of warm water for a long time before she washed my hair, and carefully rinsed it so no soap went into my eyes.

She knelt down beside me while I said my prayers and then tucked me into the wide bed and drew the curtains together, making the room darker.

"Good night, Peg—sleep well," she said, closing the door behind her.

After she left the room, I sat up, feeling afraid of the dark and the unfamiliar silence.

It didn't seem like much time had passed when the door creaked open and Mrs. Hanley looked in.

"Are ya alright, Peg?"

I didn't answer her, because I didn't want her to know I was crying. She came over and sat on the edge of the bed. Her soft hand wiped my cheeks dry and she swept a stray hair off of my face.

"Slide over, I'll lie down with ya, till ya fall asleep."

I did as she said and the weight of her body beside me felt comforting and I quickly fell asleep.

When I woke up in the morning, Mrs. Hanley was gone, but the door had been left ajar. I crept out of the room and stood where the hallway opened into the kitchen. The table was set for two and Mrs. Hanley was stirring something in a pot on the electric cooker.

"Well, good morning, Peg! I hope yer hungry. I've made us some porridge."

She filled our bowls with warm, thick, creamy yellow porridge and swirled in a spoonful of jam. She told me I wouldn't see Mr. Hanley in the mornings because he leaves early to go to work at Merlin Park Hospital. We ate together and then she told me to wash up and put on one of the frocks she'd left on the bed. One was blue and the other green, both made from a light, soft material. I put on the green one and she was pleased to see how well it fit. She said her sister, Hannah, sent them over from America, which made them extra special.

We went to Boot's Chemist Shoppe in the city center, where she bought me hair clips and a bag of sweets. I unrolled one of the pinwheels, stretched out the long lace of liquorish, and ate it slowly as we walked over to Eyre Square. When I finished eating the third one, Mrs. Hanley urged me to join the other children and I shyly walked over to them.

After a short while, one of the girls tugged me and said, "Yer mam is callin ya."

I looked up to see Mrs. Hanley beckoning me over to her; the girl thought she was my mother. I said good bye and ran over to Mrs. Hanley, placing my hand in hers, then turning to wave to my new friends.

Back at the house later in the day, I sat at the table watching Mrs. Hanley fix supper at the counter. While she cut the vegetables, she told me stories about living on the farm. That made me think of the Clearys, and I remembered her visiting there more than once.

"Was Mrs. Cleary yer friend?"

She put down the knife and looked at the floor for a moment before answering.

"Not really, well sort of. I mean I knew the Cleary family, but we weren't really friends."

"Mrs. Cleary isn't my mam, ya know."

"I know that," she replied quickly.

"Do ya know her? My mam? Do ya know who she is?"

Mrs. Hanley picked up a dish towel, and twisted it in her hands as she came over and sat across from me. She seemed preoccupied for a few moments, spreading the towel out on the table and flattening it with her hands.

"Peg, when I found ya in the barn and took ya back to Moycullen, I wanted ta keep ya. But I just couldn't do that."

"Ya mean, keep me like the Clearys, as a foster child?"

Mrs. Hanley paused, and took a deep breath.

"Well, yes, sort of, but it wouldn't have worked."

"Was it because of that man? Yer pa?"

"Oh no, Peg, it's hard ta explain. I'd just started courtin Dan, and Hannah was leavin fer America."

I nodded, but I really didn't understand what she was saying. I didn't want to know about those people.

"But Mrs. Hanley, do ya know who my mam is?"

She folded the dish towel, stood up, walked over to the sink and looked out the window.

"No Peg, I don't know who yer mam is."

After I climbed into bed, Mrs. Hanley lay down beside me again, and this time she put an arm over me. I felt a little restricted, but it really didn't bother me, and I liked the way she smelled and it felt nice having her close to me.

In the morning after breakfast, I put on the blue frock and Mrs. Hanley put the matching clips in my hair. I admired myself in the mirror, and was glad that no one could tell that I was one of the house children. Skipping down the hill ahead of her, I was excited to get to the park to play with the children. Mrs. Hanley sat on a bench and watched me run over to the girl I'd played with yesterday.

"Hi, Peg," she greeted me. "I like yer hair clips."

I leaned in toward her and responded in a low voice, "Thanks, my mam bought em fer me."

When we returned to the house, Mrs. Hanley washed the laundry in a tub and I handed her the pins as she hung the clothing on a line. I noticed her looking at the number 27 marked in my jumper.

"That's my number."

"I know," she said. "I was 15."

"You were in Saint Thomas?"

She shook her head no. "No, no, I wasn't there. Never mind."

When Mr. Hanley came home that evening he was as jolly as ever.

"Do ya know yer horses, Peg?" he asked.

"The only horse I ever knew was Ginger from the Cleary's," I said.

"Well, ya've got ta know yer horses, Peg," he said. "This is race week in Galway and we're goin ta place a bet. Tell me Peg, which one is goin ta be the winner? Will it be Devil Diver, Sleepy Fox, Ticino, Brown Jack, Kelso . . ."

I laughed at all the silly names.

"I'd say Sleepy Fox is goin ta be the winner," I said.

"Sleepy Fox it is then!"

∞

The following morning, a crashing sound woke me and I jumped out of bed and rushed into the kitchen. Mrs. Hanley was on her knees picking up the pieces of a shattered dish.

"Peg, go sit down while I clean this up," she said.

I sat by the fireplace and noticed something different about her—and it made me feel uneasy. She gave me breakfast, but she didn't sit with me and she didn't talk to me—and every few minutes she looked out the window, as if she were waiting for someone.

I got dressed, went out to the yard and looked through the bushes at the children playing. I'd just picked up a stone to toss over the hedge when I noticed a woman standing at the back door. Her gray hair was pulled back in a bun and she wore round, wire-rimmed glasses.

"Come on over here, let me get a good look at ya."

I was a little nervous; but did as she said, and as I got closer, I recognized her as Mrs. Hanley's mam.

"I'm Peg," I said.

"Call me Granny, that's what all the children call me."

"Hi, Granny," I said.

"I hear yer doin well in school."

"I am, and I made my First Holy Communion."

"So I've heard. Do ya know yer rosary?"

"Yes, I do. We say it every night."

She nodded with approval, then turned around and went back into the house. I listened by the door, but couldn't hear anything.

∞

After Granny left, Mrs. Hanley called me in and she seemed more like herself again. She told me her mam visits every Wednesday and Saturday after selling eggs and milk at the market.

I helped her put away the goods Granny had brought over and then we went into town. She bought me a sweet bun and we sat on a bench across from the Great Southern Hotel, a stately inn busy with tourists visiting for the races. We watched them come and go and shared a few good laughs critiquing their fancy clothes and outrageous hats.

"You'd think they were in the films!" she said, referring to the men wearing bright summer suits and matching top hats.

Later we joked about the hat styles we'd like to wear ourselves and laughed as we conjured up the perfect suit and hat for Mr. Hanley to wear for his film debut.

He was in an equally good mood when he came home.

He waved a card in his hand and asked, "Peg, do ya know what this is?"

"No, I don't."

"It's a race card, and this one's a winner!" he exclaimed. "Yer call on Sleepy Fox was on the money!"

Both of the Hanleys seemed very happy about this and I was glad that I'd picked a good horse.

"Peg, I've got a little somethin fer ya," he said. "How'd ya like a banana?"

"I've never had a banana."

"Well then, it's high time ya did!"

Mr. Hanley unfolded his newspaper and removed the odd-look-
ing yellow fruit. I watched him peel back the thick skin from the stem,
revealing the white pulp inside. It tasted sweet and delicious and after
my last bite I said I'd be happy to pick another horse for him. He let
out a hearty infectious laugh and Mrs. Hanley and I joined him.

Before going to bed, I said good night to him and he gently patted
me on the head.

"You know what, Peg? I think yer my lucky charm."

As I lay in bed that night, with the warmth of Mrs. Hanley beside
me and the thought of being Mr. Hanley's lucky charm, I knew I
wanted to stay here.

Thursday morning after breakfast, Mrs. Hanley gave me a pair of
short pants and a sleeveless top to wear.

"We're goin ta the strand!" she said.

I suddenly realized that I hadn't thought about the house children or the trip to the beach that I'd missed.

Mrs. Hanley packed ham sandwiches and a jug of lemonade into
a sack and took a large blanket from the press. At Eyre Square we met
her friend Delia and her two daughters—Evelyn, a year older than
me, and Regan, my age. We boarded the bus for Salt Hill and I sat in
between the girls, and Mrs. Hanley and Delia sat behind us.

It was a short ride to the little beach town lined with pastel-col-
ored shoppes. The bus pulled up in front of a big white building with
a sign that read, "Hawthorn Lodge."

In a single line, we walked down a long, narrow path leading to
the beach. I looked ahead at the waves crashing into the shoreline
and took off my sandals, letting my feet sink into the soft, grainy
sand.

Mrs. Hanley fed us and then we ran down to the water, where I cautiously wet my feet. The bay was cold, and when Regan splashed me, it tasted salty. We played on the beach all afternoon and were wiped out when it was time to leave.

At the house, I collapsed into a green chair while Mrs. Hanley busied herself in the kitchen.

I was about to fall asleep when Mr. Hanley came barreling through the front door.

"It looks like the beach wiped ya out, Peg!"

I smiled and nodded.

I could barely finish my meal and when we were done, I asked Mrs. Hanley if I could go to bed.

"Of course ya can, Peg. The sun and salt water will do that ta ya."

Mrs. Hanley laid down next to me. My last thought before falling asleep was that she had to be the nicest lady in the world.

∞

Mrs. Hanley was making bread when I came into the kitchen the following morning. She placed the dough into the black pot, and I looked at her curiously as she cut a cross onto the loaf before placing the lid on top.

"Tis ta bless the bread and give thanks."

I nodded and smiled at her, thinking what a great mam she'd be and wondered why she didn't have any children.

The day passed easily in her company. We strolled through the city talking and laughing, and when we stopped in Saint Nicholas' Church she gave me a halfpenny to light a candle. I knelt down and prayed to God, thanking him for my holiday and asking him to let me stay.

That night, I offered to set the table, and as I took the dishes from the cupboard, I looked at the photographs on display. Mrs. Hanley came up behind me and pointed to a picture of three girls and a boy.

"Twas the last time we were all together," she said. "That's my older brother, Martin, my older sister Margaret, Hannah, and me. We used ta have great fun, but now they're all in America."

I could hear the sadness in her voice.

The following morning I was surprised to see Mr. Hanley sitting at the table drinking a cup of tea.

"It's Saturday, Peg, and it's my day off."

Mrs. Hanley spooned porridge into the three bowls on the table.

"My mam will be comin by again today, Peg."

"She told me ta call her Granny."

"Did she?"

Mr. and Mrs. Hanley exchanged a look of surprise.

I was lost in a daydream, pretending I lived with the Hanleys, when Granny came through the door. She didn't knock. She just walked right in and placed two baskets on the table. One was full of eggs and the other held two jars of milk. Mrs. Hanley went to the sink to fill the kettle and Granny turned to me.

"Will ya be havin tea with us, Peg?"

I looked over at Mrs. Hanley and she smiled and nodded.

"Yes, I will," I said.

Mrs. Hanley emptied the basket and set the table while Granny questioned me.

"Are ya any good at yer sums?"

"I am," I said, "but I prefer readin."

"Yer sums are important," said Granny. "Let me see yer hand."

She took my hand and stuck something in my palm—it was a sixpence coin. My eyes nearly popped out of my head.

"Is this fer me?"

"'Tis."

"I've never had any money before."

"When ya get back ta school, pay attention ta yer sums."

"I will, Granny. Thank you."

I turned the coin over in my hand as the two women chatted. Granny finished her tea and looked toward me before getting up to leave.

"Now Peg, remember what I told ya—mind yer sums!"

Mrs. Hanley seemed relieved when Granny closed the door behind her.

"Peg, today is the last day of yer holiday," she said. "Would ya like ta go back ta the park?"

"Yes, I would," I said.

I played with the children knowing it would be the last time I'd see them, and I was upset when it started to rain. Reluctantly I said goodbye, but didn't mention that I wouldn't be back.

At the house, Mrs. Hanley gave me a pencil and a sheet of paper.

"Here Peg, ya can practice yer sums."

I sat at the table and wrote out some arithmetic problems, and she settled into a chair by the fireplace and began knitting. Every now and then, she looked over at me and I wondered if she was as sad as I was about my holiday being over.

As usual, Mr. Hanley came barreling into the house with the paper under his arm.

"I think I beat the heavy rain," he said. "I could hear it comin up behind me. So Peg, yer leavin us tomorrow."

"Yes, I have ta go back," I said.

"Is it the nuns yer missin?" he asked, and then he howled with laughter.

I didn't laugh with him this time. I didn't miss the nuns or the industrial school. I wanted to stay right here with the Hanleys.

That night when Mrs. Hanley laid down next to me, I tried not to fall asleep because I didn't want the day to end.

On Sunday morning, I put on my green frock and walked between the Hanleys to Saint Nicholas' Church. During the homily the priest said some terrible things about the Galway races and Mr. Hanley looked at me with a devilish grin—I had to hold back my chuckle. We returned to the house for a big breakfast and I stuffed myself with eggs, rashers, and black pudding.

Mrs. Hanley packed my bag and I said goodbye to Mr. Hanley when it was time to leave.

"We'll see ya again, Peg," he said and handed me a banana. "Somethin ta eat on the train."

I sadly took my last look at the city as we walked to the station. We stood on the platform waiting for Sheila.

"Peg, I hope ya had a nice time."

"I did, Mrs. Hanley. Thank ya very much."

"I'll try ta come see ya."

"That would be nice," I said. "I've never had a visitor."

Before she could say anything else, Sheila came over to us and gabbed on about her holiday until the train rolled in. Mrs. Hanley gave me a hug and handed me my bag, and for a moment it looked like she was about to cry.

I knelt on the seat and held back my tears while I waved to Mrs. Hanley as the train pulled out of the station. Once the Galway Bay was out of sight, I sat back down.

"So how was yer holiday?" asked Sheila.

"Oh Sheila, it was the best!" I said. "Mr. and Mrs. Hanley are the nicest people. She cooked fer me every day and we went ta the strand and we . . ."

Sheila interrupted me.

"Peg, I'm happy fer ya, and that's all fine," she said. "But fer yer own sake, ya might not want ta be tellin the others what a grand time ya had."

I paused for a moment, thinking about what she'd said, and realized she was right.

I thanked her, and gave her half of my banana.

"Yer frock is lovely, Peg," said Sheila.

"Thanks," I said. "I've another one in my bag."

"Peg, ya know ya can't keep em. Sister Constance won't have it. She'll say ya fancy yerself, and ya can't have somethin special the other girls can't have. She likes ta keep us all the same."

As I took the last bite of my banana, I knew that Sheila was right again, and my holiday was over.

CHAPTER FOUR

I was back in farm clothes the next day, sitting in the yard that seemed even smaller than before. Going to Galway had been like visiting another world, and I yearned to return there. The most frustrating thing was keeping the details about my trip to myself, knowing that if I shared them with Mary, she would build a resentment toward me. So during the day, I acted like my holiday was no big deal, but at night in bed, I pined to return to the Hanleys' house.

The last two weeks of July were rough as I readjusted to the routine and terrible meals. Other than going to Saint Michael's for confession and taking our Sunday walk to the train station, our summer days were confined to the yard. Toward the end of the summer, Theresa, Mary's big sister, offered to teach us how to knit. We sat against the back wall with the older girls, making socks for the upcoming school year. I hated it—my black yarn was always hopelessly twisting in knots—but I enjoyed being around the older girls. One afternoon, as Theresa tried to untangle my mess, Sheila came over to talk to us.

"Did ya hear? A slew of girls are comin in from Saint Joe's in Cavan."

"Why are they comin here?" Theresa asked.

"Somethin about a fire burnin down their dorms."

During supper everyone was whispering about it.

"Twas a terrible fire!"

"Some of em got killed!"

"The bloody nuns locked em up in the dorms and they couldn't get out."

"Twasn't the Mercy nuns, twas the Poor Clares!"

⚭

That evening, during the rosary, I spotted the Cavan girls sitting together in a back corner of the rec room. After we finished praying, Sister Constance read out new bed and job assignments for everyone. I'd be cleaning her staircase banister with number 6.

Mary motioned toward the Cavan girls. "Ya must be workin with one of em, 6 was Bridget's number."

I walked over to the sullen group and asked who was number 6. A tall, thin girl, with long, dark hair hanging in her face, came forward from the back of the crowd. She nervously pushed the hair out of her eyes and introduced herself as Joan. She thanked me for coming over and said she'd look for me at breakfast.

Up in the dorms, the girls moved their belongings to their new bed assignments. A set of twins, Blackie and Brownie Burns, were assigned to the beds to my left. They'd arrived a few weeks ago and I didn't know them well. Blackie was very bossy over her sister, and when she left the room I went over to talk to Brownie.

"Why is she always tellin ya what ta do?"

Brownie smiled and said, "Aw, it's just her way. She thinks she has ta care fer me, cause our mam is too sick to watch us."

It was the first night I didn't think about Galway. More girls than usual were crying, and I figured it was the girls from Cavan and tried to imagine what it was like for them.

The next morning Joan sat across from Mary and me in the refectory and told us about the fire.

"Twas terrible. The heat was unbearable, and flames were comin up through the floor from the laundry."

She pushed the hair off her face, leaned across the table and whispered, "The locals were outside yellin fer the nuns ta open the door, and Sister Amelia ignored them, tellin us ta go upstairs."

"Why didn't she open the door?"

"She didn't want us goin outside in our sleepin gowns."

Mary looked at her skeptically, "Then how'd ya get out?"

"My sister Aisling pushed Sister Amelia ta the floor, grabbed her key and unlocked the door. Twas sheer panic!"

"Where's yer sister now?"

"I don't know, they split us up and shipped us ta different places."

While I diligently worked my way down the staircase, polishing my side of the banister, Joan rambled on about the fire, even though we weren't supposed to be talking. Out in the yard I complained about working with her and Mary warned me, "Ya better tell her ta shut her trap or ya'll both be gettin the strap!"

On the first day of Primary School, I was anxious to get our job done quickly, and Joan was taking her time, talking away. We were about halfway down the stairwell when I heard the door from Saint Luke's Parlor open and the familiar clinking sound of wooden beads hitting a leather strap. I kicked Joan to get her attention and then saw Sister Constance looking up at us from the bottom of the steps. With our rags in our hands, we stood up together and greeted her.

She began to climb the stairs, and we stepped to the side so she could pass between us. When she reached our step she stopped, and without warning she whipped her arm around and smacked Joan across the face. Joan dropped her rag and her eyes welled up with tears. Then, a moment later, Sister Constance turned to me and swung her enormous hand across my face. She hit me so hard that my ears started to ring. I lifted the oily rag in my hand to my cheek to cool the sting. Sister Constance pointed her big finger at Joan's rag on the step and said, "Pick that up and get back to work."

Mary's eyes widened when I met her in the yard before going to class.

"The side of yer face is all red!"

I tried to cover my cheek with my hair as we walked into our new classroom. Catherine smiled and waved to me, motioning for me take the seat next to her. Her pretty pink dress reminded me of the ones I wore in Galway and I wished that I was wearing one of them now.

Our Second Class teacher, Sister Vincent, was a soft-spoken nun, known for her leniency. Each morning, before our lesson, she allowed us ample time to settle in and speak briefly with our classmates. In October, while the townsfolk were setting up for the fair, she let us look out of the window each day to see their progress.

On the Saturday we'd be attending the fair, Mary laid out our plans for the day while we ate breakfast.

"I think we should go right ta the games, then we'll go see the animals and maybe stop ta watch the dancers."

I nodded my head in agreement. "The rides and games'll get crowded fast."

With our tickets in our hands, we raced to the amusement area and selected our cars on the Dodgem Track, ready to bump into all the other cars as soon as the vendor flipped the control switch. A blonde-headed girl sat in the empty car behind Mary. It was Catherine! When the ride started, we both drove into Mary, causing her car to jerk back and forth several times before she managed to get away from us. Mary was so mad, and when the ride was over, she let me know about it.

"What's the matter with ya? We're not supposed ta be mixen with the town's children."

The following Saturday, we were in the yard knitting when I heard someone calling my name. Mary poked me and pointed upwards. Catherine was looking down at us over the wall. She held out an apple and asked if I wanted it. I jumped up and raised my hands to catch it, but it went over my head, and another girl swooped it off the ground. Catherine disappeared and the girl with my apple gave me a sneering look before biting into it.

Catherine reappeared and called down to me again, "Hey Peg."

She tossed down another apple, and this time I caught it; but a taller girl grabbed it out of my hand. Catherine threw a third one down, this time aiming it at the head of the tall girl eating my apple. Several girls began to gather at the base of the wall, chanting, "Apples, apples, apples!"

Catherine disappeared again, but the mob grew and their mantra got louder. Mary and I moved away from the commotion and when I looked back, Catherine was on top of the wall dumping a basketful of apples into the yard. The girls began fighting—pulling hair, punching each other, trying to grab as many apples as they could. We stood back, not wanting to be pulled into the mayhem. Sister Constance came into the yard and rushed toward the crowd, swinging a stick and hitting anyone within her reach, and the ruckus came to a halt.

"Drop them, now! All of them!" yelled Sister Constance. "You're like a bunch of tinkers!"

She scanned the crowd with her steely eyes. "Who's responsible for this?"

Several girls looked my way, and one of them pointed at me. "It's her fault."

Sister Constance turned to face me, and Mary took a side-step to put some distance between us. I was terrified as she approached me, my eyes on the stick in her hand.

"It wasn't me, Sister Constance," I trembled in my defense. "'Twas my classmate that threw em down."

"Your classmate?"

"Yes, my friend, Catherine O'Meara."

"Your friend? Catherine O'Meara is not your friend!"

I didn't respond.

"There is no flirting with the town children!"

Sister Constance turned to face the crowd behind her.

"You are house children, and it is strictly forbidden for you to mingle with the town's children."

She turned back to me. "Do you understand?"

"Yes, Sister Constance."

Katie shuffled out to the yard with an empty basket and Sister Constance told her to have the apples picked up and sent to the barn for the animals. Then she glared at me and shook her head.

"This is what happens when you let girls go on holiday. They come back here forgetting who they are."

∞

After that incident, Sister Vincent changed my seat; an extra desk had been added to the last row, where I'd sit with the other house children. It was a terrible week for me, and I knew everyone was talking about what had happened. During my confession, I told the priest that I'd been responsible for the fighting in the yard and felt better after saying penance; but I still didn't understand what going on holiday had to do with any of it.

A friendship between Blackie, Brownie, and I began to blossom after I learned they were from Galway. They didn't know the Hanleys, but they were familiar with Eyre Square and the shoppes in town.

It was pouring rain on a Saturday afternoon in November, and Sister Constance let us stay inside, so Brownie and I sat in the rec room having one of our Galway chats. Katie surprised us and let us use the gramophone so we could sing and dance. Brownie was a great dancer, and I tried to copy her, putting my hands on my hips and then waving them up in the air. When she dropped to the floor and started twisting and shaking, I thought she was playing around; but suddenly, her eyes rolled back in her head and white foam started oozing from her mouth. I knelt down beside her and screamed for help, and the other girls stepped back, forming a circle around us. Blackie came right over, and Katie ran out of the room. I thought Brownie was dead until I saw she was peeing, so I stood up and took a step back. Katie returned with Sister Constance and the two of them picked up Brownie by her limbs. Before leaving the room, Sister Constance sent one of the girls into town to get Dr. Green and told Blackie to clean up the pee.

When Blackie finished mopping the floor, someone put the music back on, but only one girl got up to dance. She fell to the floor and started imitating Brownie, and Blackie ran over and started kicking the girl violently. I stepped out in the hallway and flicked the light switch when I saw Dr. Green and Sister Constance heading toward me. Sister Constance looked at me questioningly and I told her I had to use the lavatory. As I walked away I overheard Dr. Green talking.

"If she has another seizure, someone should press her tongue down with a stick or a spoon so she doesn't choke ta death."

The following day, I pinched a spoon during breakfast and gave it to Blackie.

Classes came to an end in December, and I was distressed to learn that a few girls were sent home for the holiday. When Mary asked me what was wrong, I told her that I'd wished Mrs. Hanley had asked for me to come and spend Christmas with them.

"Yer lucky ya went in the summer. Twas just three or four girls that went for Christmas! And they went home to their families."

I felt she didn't understand.

"The Hanleys don't have children, I could be their child!"

"People want their own, not some house child."

I tried to make the best of the Christmas celebration, but my thoughts kept returning to the Hanleys and my fantasy of living with them.

In January, the weather was cold and wet when we returned to our classes. Mary and I linked arms and ran up the lane, jumping over icy puddles to keep our feet dry. During class, I'd look with envy at the rubber boots some of the town's children wore. We'd just be rid of the chill in our bones, and the announcement would come over the speaker, "House children stand. House children go."

Our spirits waned during the damp and wintry cold months of February and March. Unless it was raining, our free time was spent outside, huddled in groups to stay warm. We looked forward to April, which would bring us the celebration of Easter and warmer days.

It was during one of those warmer days when we were called inside on a Saturday afternoon and sent to the rec room. Katie weighed and measured each one of us, and Sister Xavier updated our records. Later that same week, some of the girls were held back from class to help organize and clean, while others were fitted for new issues of clothing. I finally learned what was going on one morning.

"They're gettin ready fer inspections."

"At least we'll be eatin good fer a day or two."

"Tis all a big show!"

"Let me get a word with the inspector; I'll tell her what's goin on in here."

Sure enough, the following week, a professional-looking woman toured the Primary School with Reverend Mother Bernard, the Mother Superior in charge of the nuns and the facilities they ran in Ballinasloe. They came to our classroom and Ellen and I were asked to stand and recite part of our lesson aloud. When we were done, the inspector wrote something on her clipboard before leaving the room.

We were given a hearty helping at mealtime and the inspector looked pleased when she came out of the kitchen with Sister Constance and Sister Virginia.

The girls rolled their eyes and dug into their meal, while sharing what they knew.

"That's Dr. Walsh, she's the inspector from the government."

"She's the one who approves the headage count fer the nuns' payment."

"Payment fer what?"

"Fer carin fer us!"

Even though it wasn't Tuesday, we had a singing lesson with Sister

Angela and the inspector was there to listen, and in the evening, she saw us get served bread with butter and jam instead of drippins. That night when we went up to the dorms, Katie and Julia were pulling white spreads off all the beds.

The next day, everything was back to normal, until Sister Constance summoned me in from the yard.

"You have a visitor in Saint Luke's Parlor. I've given permission for you to go into town for a few hours."

"Thank you, Sister Constance."

"Peg, I expect you'll be on your best behavior, and don't let this privilege go to your head."

She didn't tell me who my visitor was, but I walked as fast as I could, without running, down the hall to Saint Luke's. Through the glass door, I could see her. It was Mrs. Hanley! We greeted each other with smiles and she gave me a warm hug. I held her hand as we left the building and walked into town, and I hoped that one of my classmates would see me. It was a warm, sunny day, and it felt like I was on holiday in Galway, except for my clothes, but I didn't care. We looked in the shoppe windows and admired the lovely floral patterns on the dishes, and we went into Phelan's Sweet Shoppe and bought a bag of caramels. Then we went into Saint Michael's Church and lit a candle, and I thanked God for her visit. The time went by quickly and I tried to walk slowly as we headed back, but I could see Mrs. Hanley was in a hurry.

"I've got ta catch the 3:40 train."

We said goodbye in Saint Luke's Parlor, and even though it was bold of me, before she left, I had to ask her, "Mrs. Hanley, will I be seein ya again?"

She patted me on the head. "Of course, Peg, we'll see ya again fer holiday in the summer."

As she walked out the door, I ran over to the window and watched her rush down the path. She looked back and we waved to each other. When she was out of sight, I sat down on a chair in the parlor and felt like crying, but didn't. If Sister Constance saw me crying, she might not allow Mrs. Hanley to visit me again.

Knowing I'd be going back to stay with the Hanleys in Galway for holiday lifted my spirits, and the rest of the school year didn't go by fast enough for me.

CHAPTER FIVE

Many of the girls dreaded the end of the school year, but I was thrilled when it finally arrived. The first few weeks of the summer lagged as I waited to hear the announcement about summer holiday. Even though Mrs. Hanley said I was going to Galway, until Sister Constance called my number, I couldn't be sure.

When I showed the girls my train ticket, Blackie said it wasn't fair, but Brownie said it didn't matter, because they'd be back in Galway soon enough. As expected, Mary made another snide remark. "It's only a week. I don't know what the big deal is!"

I packed my things and included my communion medal, holding onto the bit of hope that the Hanleys might decide to keep me.

At the station, I was the only girl on the westbound platform. The others were all going east. During the train ride, I thought about things to do that might make the Hanleys really like me. I got excited when the sparkling blue water finally came into view. As the train pulled into the station, I looked for Mrs. Hanley on the platform.

She greeted me with a big hug and asked, "Peg, where's yer friend?"

"She turned fifteen, and the nuns sent her on to her situation. She's working fer some family."

Mrs. Hanley brought her hands up to her face and gasped, "Peg, yer only seven years old! The nuns let ya travel all alone?"

She held my hand and carried my bag as we walked through town and I felt good to be back in Galway. I thought about Blackie and Brownie when we passed Eyre Square and told Mrs. Hanley about them.

"Peg, do you mean the Burns twins? They're in Saint Thomas' with you?"

"They're in my class. They said their mam is sick, but when she's better, they'll be sent back ta her."

Mrs. Hanley closed her eyes and shook her head.

"Oh, Peg, their mam passed away two days ago. They're burying her this morning."

It looked like my holiday was going to be much like last year. Mrs. Hanley had the table set for tea and two new dresses for me to wear. She prepared a delicious supper and I helped her set the table. When Mr. Hanley came home, he ribbed me about the nuns again, and I laughed extra hard. At bedtime, when Mrs. Hanley lay down next to me, an intense feeling of comfort overwhelmed me, and I don't know why, but tears started welling up in my eyes.

Mrs. Hanley seemed pleased the following morning while I watched her make bread. There was something about her hands that captivated me. She gently kneaded the dough with rhythm, moving her hands as if they were dancing, until the dough was smooth.

"I think yer bread tastes so good because ya make it with love."

"Why Peg, that's the nicest thing anyone has ever said to me."

I wanted to be useful and offered to polish the floor moldings, but Mrs. Hanley let out a little giggle and said that wasn't necessary.

When her daily chores were done, she'd take me to town or to the park, and one day we stopped in Saint Nicholas' Church to light a candle for Mrs. Burns.

Even though I didn't know her, I felt sad she died, and Mrs. Hanley tried to comfort me.

"Mrs. Burns needs to rest peacefully in heaven. Peg, she was very ill and suffering. This is best for her."

"But what about Blackie and Brownie?"

"The nuns'll take good care of em."

Granny came to visit on Wednesday and brought a chicken for us.

"We've got ta fatten up Peg!" she said.

While we drank tea, she asked me about my lessons in school.

"I'm doing well, Granny. I'm good with my sums, and one of the best at readin."

I'd noticed Mrs. Hanley wasn't as tense in Granny's presence this time.

We met Delia and her daughters for a trip to the beach, and it was more fun than last year. This time, Mrs. Hanley came into the water and splashed around with us. She didn't mind when we splashed her back, and she looked lovely when she threw her head back and laughed. During the ride home, Regan and Evelyn fell asleep, and I closed my eyes while listening to Mrs. Hanley and Delia whisper in the seat behind us.

"It's grand that ya have her here, even if it's just fer the week."

"Tis. It took some finagling, though. I told Dan that Mother Superior asked me ta take her."

"And Dan knows who she is?"

I couldn't hear Mrs. Hanley's response and didn't know what to make of their conversation.

The following day, Mrs. Hanley took me to a shoppe and asked if I'd prefer clips or a ribbon for my hair.

"I don't know. Whatever ya think is best'll be fine."

"Well, ya must have a preference."

I shrugged my shoulders, unfamiliar with being given a choice. I didn't want to give the wrong answer.

"Well, what's yer favorite color?"

Again, I shrugged my shoulders. I'd never thought about preferring one color over another.

Mrs. Hanley was disturbed by my reluctance to make a decision.

"Peg, ya've gotta know what ya like. Sure, ya must have a preference."

"I'll take a yellow ribbon," I said, hoping that would please her.

After working at the market on Saturday, Granny stopped in for tea.
I sat at the table chatting with her, and she admired my new hair
ribbon. Before leaving, she put another sixpence in my palm and
told me to do well at school. I liked her, not because of the money,
but because even though she had lots of questions, none of them
were about where I lived. After she left, we went to the park, and
Mrs. Hanley took a seat on the bench and I played with the children.
While I ran around a boy pulled the ribbon from my hair and ran off
with it.

"Go on and get it back," said one of the girls.

I didn't know what to do, fearing both the aggressive boy and the
possibility that Mrs. Hanley might be mad at me for letting him take
it. I looked over at her and she was busy talking to another woman, so
I threw myself to the ground, causing my knees and dress to get dirty.
She spotted me as I got up and came rushing over. I forced some tears
and told her I collided with a boy and fell down, and somehow lost
the ribbon. To my surprise, the incident didn't make her angry at all;
instead, she was extra nice to me.

I didn't want to go to sleep that night, since Sunday morning meant
my holiday was over. I lay in bed, feeling the warmth of Mrs. Hanley's
body beside me and inhaling her scent. She thought I had fallen
asleep and left the room, but I just lay there and cried and cried until
I had no more tears.

In the morning I put on my gray farm clothes, but Mrs. Hanley
insisted I change into one of the dresses.

"I want ya ta look nice fer church this morning."

"But the nuns will take it away."

"It's okay, Peg, I want ya ta wear it."

I changed into the dress and we went to mass. It was hard for me to pray after communion because I was mad at God and couldn't understand why he didn't let me stay here. We returned to the house after mass for breakfast, and while we ate, Mr. Hanley told me to tell the nuns he was asking for them. Mrs. Hanley was upset with him for saying that and told me he was joking, but he winked at me and handed me a banana.

"A little somethin in case ya get hungry on the train."

I felt sad as we walked to the station, and I think Mrs. Hanley felt the same, because we didn't talk. While we waited for the train, she asked an old woman, who was traveling to Dublin, to keep an eye on me. We said goodbye and the old woman followed me onto the train and sat down beside me. I waved to Mrs. Hanley as the train pulled out of the station. The old woman asked me why I was in Galway and I told her the Hanleys were my relations whom I visited every summer.

I got off the train in Ballinasloe and slowly walked back to the industrial school alone. I put my medal back in my cubby and went up to the dorm to change into my farm clothes.

On my way out to the yard, I ran into Brownie coming out of the bathroom. Her eyes were red-rimmed, and I could see she had been crying.

"This mornin Sister Constance told us that we wouldn't be goin home cause our mam died, and Blackie says she's lyin, but I think it's true."

"It's a terrible thing if your mam did die," I said, "but at least ya got ta know her and ya have good memories of her."

I didn't tell her that I knew it was true.

Out in the yard, I was surprised to see a new set of iron steps leading up to our dorms. My friends were excited to tell me about them.

"It's a fire escape, they put it in while you were gone."

"Must have somethin ta do with the inspection we had."

"And the fire in Cavan."

"We're havin a practice drill every Sunday morning."

Things at the industrial school shook up a bit at the end of August. Most of the nuns had left for a retreat at their convent in Spiddal. I'd seen five black cars pick them up when I came back from confession at Saint Michael's. Katie and Julia were left in charge, and that resulted in chaos. After a few days like that, I welcomed back our routine and the start of the school year.

Sister Madeline, our Third Class teacher, stood at the door waiting for us as we approached her. She was a short, hefty woman, with dark eyes and thick black eyebrows, and her voice sounded husky, like a man's. We'd been warned by the older girls that she was tough.

"House children to the back of the room," she said as we entered the classroom.

She slammed the door closed behind us, and Mary and I took seats at a desk in the last row. Sister Madeline took attendance, and then announced that physical education had been added to the curriculum this year. She also told us that it was a mandate from the Education Department that she disagreed with.

She distributed wooden dowels to us from a barrel by the door, and then took us out to the school yard. She put us in four rows and stood before our class, wrapped her sausage-like fingers around a dowel, and raised it over her head. It was difficult to keep from laughing as we followed her movements.

A small group of priests, escorted by the Reverend Mother, appeared at the back door of the school and stood there watching us. When Sister Madeline noticed their presence, she told us to continue the routine, but she put her dowel down. Brownie was next to me and fell to the ground, it looked like she was having a seizure again. I didn't know what to do, but Blackie came right over and put the spoon in her mouth, and suddenly Sister Constance was at her side, too. She ordered two girls to carry Brownie back to the industrial school.

"Father Doyle doesn't need to see this! Get her out of here!"

∞

When we returned to the classroom, Sister Madeline didn't say anything about Brownie—she just started writing arithmetic problems on the chalkboard. A girl in front of me asked me what had happened, and as I leaned forward to tell her, Sister Madeline turned around and saw me talking.

"Up front, now!"

I looked at the floor, and I knew that everyone was looking at me as I went to the front of the class. Sister Madeline grabbed me by the ear and pulled me forward, and my face reddened with embarrassment. My nose was inches away from the multiplication problems, and to my right I saw her take a dowel from the barrel. She smashed the wooden rod into the back of my knees, and I almost fell to the floor. I took a deep breath and straightened up, preparing for the next hit. She paused for a moment between each smack, but as hard as it was, I refused to cry. After striking me for the fifth time, she told me to go sit down, and then she turned back to the class.

"There will be absolutely no talking, unless I call on you!"

I gingerly eased back into my chair, careful not to let the back of my knees make contact with anything. The rest of the morning was a blur; the pain kept me from concentrating. When we went back to the refectory at noon, Mary looked at the back of my legs.

"Why didn't ya cry? That's all she wanted, then she would've stopped!"

I knew Mary was right, and it might have been foolish of me, but I didn't want to cry for that mean, fat nun.

I was concerned about Brownie, and she was nowhere in sight. On the way back to class for the afternoon session I talked to Blackie. She thanked me for the spoon and told me she'd heard that Brownie was up in the dorm.

During supper, I sat on the edge of the bench, careful not to let the back of my knees brush up against it. There was a lot of whispering around the table about a visiting priest.

"They say he's goin ta be a saint!"

"He's on the radio in America."

"They call him the Rosary Priest."

I wondered to myself if he could give Brownie a blessing and cure her.

Sister Constance, accompanied by a young priest, came into the rec room when it was time for us to say the rosary. She introduced him as Father Doyle. He was a handsome, well-built man, with broad shoulders and a full head of reddish hair swept to the side. He knelt down in front of the room and his gentle smile and lyrical voice made the rosary sound like a beautiful song. The sting in the back of my knees made it hurt to kneel, but as we prayed, I forgot about the pain. There was something about Father Doyle's voice—it was beautiful and sounded very holy. For the first time, the rosary had some meaning to me and I could see Father Doyle was a very special priest.

Up in the dorm, I was glad to see Brownie was fast asleep in her bed. That night I prayed to God to help Brownie get well, and then I prayed for myself, to be sent to live with the Hanleys.

It took several days for the burn behind my knees to go away and even longer for the welts to heal. In class, I concentrated on the lessons and didn't say a word, even if someone else spoke to me.

In October the cooler weather of autumn arrived, and Mary and I ran through the Ballinasloe Fair like we owned it. We didn't feel like the little ones anymore, and we started talking about jumping the gate the next time the opportunity came around.

When November arrived, the weather quickly turned bitter cold. Ireland's dampness settled in my bones and I prayed for a good, warm coat. Dr. Green was coming to the industrial school weekly because so many girls were ill. Even the town's children were missing class; some of them had clothes no warmer than ours. Sister Madeline said there was a bad bout of consumption. Three girls in my dorm were sent to the hospital with TB, and we never heard about them or saw them again.

Christmas wasn't much fun that year. Sister Angela got sick, and no one decorated the rec room, but at least we had our special meal. All I thought about was getting warm and wondering what the Hanleys were doing. Once again, I wished that I could've spent the holiday with them.

When we returned to school in January, many of the children were still out sick. I think Sister Madeline and I were the only ones that didn't get ill that winter, and she began to take a liking to me. Whenever she called on me in class, I knew the answer.

As spring approached I wondered if Mrs. Hanley would visit again, like she had the year before. But the only thing that came to me that spring was the nits. Almost everyone had them and Dr. Green sent over an ointment to be put into our hair. Angela, the girl with the long, lovely red hair from the laundry, used a metal comb on my head to get them out.

"Why don't you have em?"

"I get in the tub before the rest of ye. It's a benefit from workin in the laundry."

"I'm mad with the itch!"

"Well don't let the nuns hear ya complainin. They shaved Rose's head this mornin."

I didn't know who Rose was, but I spotted her in the refectory. The poor girl was shaved bald.

After that day, Mary and I got to the head of the line on bath days.

June arrived and there was still no sign of Mrs. Hanley. I began to worry that I wouldn't be going to Galway for holiday. I fretted in the yard, and in her way, Mary tried to comfort me.

"Yer better off stayin here. Tis just a tease when they send ya out. Another way fer the nuns ta torture ya."

She was right. It felt like torture each time I had to return from Galway.

The school year ended and it was a warm day in July when the nuns left for a conference day in Dublin, providing Mary and I the opportunity we'd been waiting for. We jumped the gate and stood in the lane, unsure of what to do next. A group of girls were heading toward the orchard and we followed behind them. Theresa stopped us as we turned toward the river.

"Where ya goin?"

"Why?"

"Just warning ya, keep away from the farm and the greenhouse."

"Why?"

"Mr. Campbell's son, Mathew, is workin. He's always tryin ta get at the girls."

We had no plans to go to the farm or greenhouse and decided we'd better stay with the group.

I went to bed that night telling myself I didn't need to go to Galway. Mary and I could make our own fun. She was right, going on holiday was a tease and a form of torture.

The following day, when Sister Constance read the list of girls going on holiday, I was elated to hear my number called.

CHAPTER SIX

When the Galway Bay came into view, I pinched myself to make sure it wasn't a dream. As the train pulled into the station, I spotted Mrs. Hanley in the crowd. I ran across the platform and greeted her with a big hug, and then she motioned to the pram beside her.

"Peg, this is Ryan, our new baby boy."

My mouth opened, but no words came out, and my heart felt like it dropped into my stomach. I tried to hide my shock by looking into the pram, pretending to be curious. The baby was lying on his stomach and I couldn't see his face—there was just a head of curly blond hair.

"That's yer baby?"

Mrs. Hanley smiled and nodded. She didn't seem to notice my displeasure. As we walked through town, I wondered if he was the reason she hadn't come to visit me at the industrial school. We stopped in front of the sweet shoppe and she went inside alone. I looked into the pram again and gave the baby a poke. He squirmed a bit but didn't make a sound. I was about to pinch him when the shoppe door opened and Mrs. Hanley came out with a small bag of sweets for me.

At the house, the table was set for tea, and a freshly baked loaf of bread was cooling on the window sill.

"I'm goin ta give Ryan a bottle first. Why don't ya change inta one of the frocks I left on the bed?"

I went to the bedroom and changed my clothes. Then I sat on the bed and cried, thinking my chances for becoming part of this family had abruptly come to an end.

"How about ya burp Ryan while I put the kettle on."

"I've never held a baby before. I'm afraid."

"Don't ya worry, Peg, ya'll do fine. Gently pat him on the back."

She put a cloth on my shoulder and placed him into my arms. He kept moving, and it was a challenge to keep him in place.

When we sat down at the table, I told Mrs. Hanley that Father Doyle had come to visit the industrial school, and she wanted to know all the details. I was thrilled to have her attention.

"He's known as the Rosary Priest. I think he's goin ta become a saint."

"Oh Peg, I know all about him! He's on the radio, ya know. He says the family that prays together, stays together."

"He has a lovely voice."

"Twas a blessin ya got ta see him. But tell me, is he as handsome as his photos?"

When Mr. Hanley came home, she had me tell him about Father Doyle's visit, but he didn't seem as impressed.

"They treat him like he's an American film star."

Mrs. Hanley took Ryan along for our walk to the cemetery. We chatted as we strolled by the rows of headstones, but she was clearly distracted. I felt a little out of place all evening, until she came in to my bedroom that night and lay down next to me. Feeling her beside me felt right, and I reached for her hand and pulled her arm over me.

In the morning, Mrs. Hanley set out a bowl of porridge for me, and then she disappeared. I'd finished my breakfast before she returned with the baby in her arms. While she fed him, I washed up and got ready to go into town.

We went to the shoppes and then stopped in Eyre Square. I ran around with the other children and Mrs. Hanley sat on a bench rocking the pram. I looked over at her a few times, but she didn't seem to notice me.

Unlike my prior visits, this time I felt very uncomfortable. I'd been used to having Mrs. Hanley to myself. One evening during supper, Mr. Hanley and I were laughing and Mrs. Hanley got upset with us.

"You two keep it down! Ryan is sleepin'!"

Mr. Hanley smirked and raised his eyebrows, but I felt like crying. I'd never seen her so angry before.

When Granny came to visit, she doted on the new baby, too. If I didn't have the story about Father Doyle, I don't think she would've talked to me.

I didn't have any fun until we went to Salt Hill with Delia and her girls. It was a big ordeal getting on and off the bus with the extra baby things, but it was worth it once we got there. We played in the sand and waded in the cool bay water. Evelyn asked me what I thought about the new baby.

"He's fine. I get ta hold him."

"Well, I hate boys."

"Why?"

"Cause they're always the favorites."

We were working on a sand castle when Mrs. Hanley called us over.

"Ryan's not feelin well, he's fussin quite a bit. It's best we get home."

Mrs. Hanley and Delia were already packing up our things.

Evelyn rolled her eyes and whispered, "Told ya, anythin ta please the boys."

During the bus ride, Regan and Evelyn told me they had an older brother and their mam favored him, and that's the way it was in everyone's house. The boys were spoiled.

While the baby took a nap, I peeled the potatoes and helped get supper ready, grateful to be spending time alone with Mrs. Hanley. After we ate, she tended to household chores and Mr. Hanley read his newspaper. I began to think that I might have been better off staying back at the industrial school with my friends. My feelings were jumbled, because when Mrs. Hanley lay down beside me in bed that night, I felt differently.

Over the next few days, our plans were continuously changing on a moment's notice, depending on how the baby was acting. Mrs.

Hanley was always trying to figure out why he was fussing and what would please him.

"Let me warm up some milk fer Ryan," Mrs. Hanley said and placed him into my arms.

I sat in the chair, unwillingly cradling him, while he cried and squirmed. His face was red and blotchy and snot was coming out of his nose. I rocked him a bit and he began to settle down.

"Ah, you've got the hang of it, why don't ya feed him?"

Reluctantly, I took the bottle and put it into his mouth. I felt a little proud that I was able to soothe him, and it pleased Mrs. Hanley, but when he was done with the bottle, he spit up all over me. I screamed, he cried, and Mrs. Hanley ran over and took him from me. I ran outside to the yard, and after a while she came out to get me.

The days dragged and I found myself feeling annoyed, bored, lonely, and anxious to get back to my friends at the industrial school. There was no way I could compete with Ryan. He was Mrs. Hanley's baby, and I was just one of the house children.

On Saturday, when the baby slept late, I had Mrs. Hanley's full attention for most of the morning. She taught me how to make bread and let me put the cross on top. I found myself feeling hopeful, but for what, I wasn't sure.

Later, when Granny arrived, Mrs. Hanley was changing the baby in the back room, so I set the table. Granny watched me butter the slices of bread and pile them on a serving dish.

"I helped make the bread today."

"Did ya? Well, that's grand, Peg, but there's more ta keepin house than that. Can ya sew?"

"No, but I can knit."

"Sewing is important, ya'll have ta learn."

"I don't know if the nuns teach that."

"It's in yer blood, ya'll learn."

I smiled and nodded, but wasn't sure what she meant by that. She seemed a bit confused, but still gave me a sixpence before she left.

I went to bed feeling fine about returning to Ballinasloe the following day, but then it happened again. Mrs. Hanley lay down next to me, and I listened to her breath and felt the warmth of her body beside me, and I wanted to stay.

Saying goodbye to Mrs. Hanley at the station had always been a special moment, and I was hurt when she asked Mr. Hanley to take me. Before I boarded the train, he pulled a banana from his pocket and gave it to me and patted me on the head.

"Somethin ta nibble on durin yer ride."

"Thank ya, Mr. Hanley."

The train whistle blew and I looked out the window to wave to him, but he was gone. During the ride, I ate my banana and wondered if that was my last visit to Galway.

I returned to the industrial school feeling glad and mad at the same time. I was glad to be with my friends again, but mad at Mrs. Hanley for having a baby. It was so confusing, because part of me loved Mrs. Hanley and a part of me hated her—well, hated that she loved her new baby so much.

It wasn't too bad getting back in to our summer routine, and I told myself that life with the Hanleys wasn't that great. I enjoyed being with my friends, and we had lots to talk about while we were knitting out in the yard, but I couldn't deny missing Mrs. Hanley's cooking.

Before the summer ended, ten girls transferred in from Goldenbridge Industrial School. Against Mary's warning, I befriended one of them, a girl our age named Maggie.

When I tried to teach Maggie how to knit, I noticed scarring on her hands.

"What happened to yer hands?"

"Tis from stringing beads."

"What do ya mean?"

"We had ta make rosary beads fer the nuns ta sell. Twas terrible, stringin the beads onta wire, sixty decades every day. Them nuns were terrible, breathin down our necks, calling us illegitimates, and the devil's handmaids. Ye've got it good here."

Listening to Maggie talk about Goldenbridge made me more appreciative of Saint Thomas'.

We were assigned new jobs at the end of the summer before returning to school. Although I'd be working alone, I felt fortunate to be polishing the banister of the main staircase in the convent. On my first day, an older girl named Erin met me in the convent foyer and showed me where to get my supplies. I'd also began to meet many of the nuns I hadn't seen before, including Sister Louise, who'd be our new teacher in Fourth Class. I was fond of her because she showed no favoritism to the town's children.

In October our singing class started up again and everyone was very surprised to hear Maggie sing. Her voice was magnificent, and Sister Angela praised her. As the weeks passed by, it became obvious that Maggie was becoming Sister Angela's pet, and many of the girls were jealous.

During breakfast one morning, Maggie took a medal out of her sock and showed it to us.

"It's Saint Celia, patron saint of music."

"Where'd ya get that?"

"Sister Angela gave it ta me."

"I wouldn't be tellin everyone about that. Keep it ta yerself."

Either someone overheard her or Maggie didn't take my advice, because later that day, Mary and I watched a group of girls surround her in the yard.

"Let's see yer fancy medal!" they chanted as they pushed her to the ground and ripped off her clothes, looking for the medal. Maggie kicked and cried, but there was nothing I could do to help her. The dinky little medal fell out when one of the girls pulled off her shoes. They passed it around until one very tall girl threw it over the wall.

"Where's yer medal now? Where's yer medal now?"

I began to think Mary was right; it was best if we kept to ourselves. Mary was my best friend, and I finally confided in her about Mrs. Hanley's new baby. In her pragmatic way, she told me I was wasting my time thinking about them. She discouraged me from entertaining any fantasies of another life, other than the real one I was living. So I tried not to think about the Hanleys or how they were celebrating Christmas with their new baby, but when I had trouble sleeping, I couldn't help but think about them.

It was one of those nights when I couldn't sleep, February 25, 1947, that Ireland got hit with the biggest blizzard of the century. The dorm windows rattled and the freezing wind penetrated the walls. In the morning, everything outside was glazed in ice and downstairs the windows were blocked by snow drifts. Ballinasloe was shut down and we all felt cold and trapped.

In the rec room, the girls talked about sleeping together to keep warm.

"Are ya sharin yer bed?"

"No, but I keep my clothes on under my sleeping gown."

"Well, don't let anyone in yer bed. Sister Constance checked our dorm last night and anyone doubled up got a thrashin."

"She said it's immoral."

We were sent out in the yard after Mr. Campbell and his son cleared a walking path. Huddled together in groups, we tried to keep warm while our hands turned blue and purple. When we were finally let back inside, Dr. Green had to be called because so many girls were complaining of swelling and itching. He said we had chilblains and left a few jars of ointment.

The cold was brutal, and I'd linger as long as possible, polishing the banister in the warm convent. While working, I listened to the nuns talk about rations until the roads could be cleared, which explained the smaller portions we'd been receiving.

We were all desperately hungry, and Mary was stunned when I

broached the idea of breaking into the pantry. It was dangerous, but I was starving and so was she.

From the dorm window I watched for the last light to go out in the convent, then took a deep breath and slid out from under my blanket. I'd kept my socks on, which made it easy to slide across the cold wooden floor without making noise. At the doorway, we glanced up and down the hall to make sure it was empty and then ran to the staircase. We hugged the wall of the dark stairwell and crept down one step at a time. The main floor was dimly lit and we rushed to the refectory door. Once inside, it was dark and still, and Mary began to panic.

"Maybe we should go back."

"No way. We've come this far!"

"What if we get caught?"

I grabbed her with one hand and placed the other on the wall and led her toward the scullery. This was new territory, and we had no idea where the food was kept. We found the pantry, but all the cabinet doors were locked. Again, Mary wanted to go back, but I refused. Together we pulled on one door until we broke the lock. The cabinet was filled with cans of fruit and boxes of red and green gelatin.

I grabbed a can of peaches in syrup. "Look at all these!"

"Put it back, we've no way of openin it!"

Mary handed me a box of red gelatin, and we took out the small blocks. I licked the hard, sweet square to soften it up, and then ate two more. As we crept back through the refectory, we heard a noise out in the hall. We hid under the table and watched two other girls come in and run across the room and into the scullery.

Over breakfast the following morning, Mary and I exchanged a knowing glance when we learned that two girls with green mouths were punished for breaking into the pantry.

∞

Three long weeks passed before the Primary School was reopened. Mr. Campbell and his son, Mathew, put wooden boards over the wet mess in the lane for us to walk on. A nun waited at the back door of the school and made us bang the mud off our shoes before entering the building. During class, I asked if the storm had hit other towns and Sister Louise said yes. I wondered if Galway was one of them. Then she said that things were getting better and deliveries of supplies were expected to arrive in Ballinasloe today.

From the window I saw a lorry full of food park on Society Street, at the end of our lane. When we were dismissed at noon, the girls ran down the lane and I pulled Mary up toward the street.

"I need ya ta hoist me up."

She lifted me onto the bed of the lorry and I tossed down ruby-red beets that she stuffed into her clothing. We escaped as the driver emerged from the convent.

By May, the lives of everyone in Ballinasloe were getting back to normal, except for one girl in my class, Patsy Doran, one of the town's children. Her mother died giving birth during the storm, her new baby brother was living with her aunt in town, and Patsy and her three sisters were sent to the industrial school. I thought of Ryan and told her that's how it is, boys are always favored.

Patsy began to pal around with us, and Mary didn't seem to mind; she said Patsy could help us since she knew her way about the town. We invited Patsy to jump the gate with us when we heard the nuns were going to Dublin.

Saturday morning, I polished my way down the banister and

said goodbye to the nuns as they left the convent carrying their black leather totes. I rushed to put my supplies away, and as I was leaving Erin called me from the china closet.

"Sister Rita wants ta see ya in the kitchen."

"I thought all the nuns went ta Dublin."

"Not the lay nuns."

I rushed down the corridor and cracked open the glass door.

"Good mornin, Sister Rita. Erin said ya wanted to see me."

"Yes, come in. I've gotta job fer ya."

She handed me a bucket of soapy water and a rag and told me to scrub down the tables in the nuns' dining room. I moved as quickly as I could, washing down the six long, white, wooden tables. When I was done, she gave me a butter sandwich that I gobbled down as I ran back to the industrial school. I scanned the yard looking for Mary and Patsy, but they were gone.

CHAPTER SEVEN

The excitement I'd felt in past years didn't surface as I packed my things for Galway. I was concerned about my absence from the industrial school for a whole week—it would give Mary and Patsy time together without me. They were forming a close friendship since they had gone into town together, and I didn't want to be excluded. I liked Patsy, but I loved Mary, and I didn't want to lose her. Mary was like a sister to me; she knew me better than anyone. Living as orphans in the industrial school required us to form our own families among ourselves. We'd been together since I arrived.

Reluctantly, I walked to the station and boarded the westbound train. I looked out of the window without noticing the passing landscape, wondering what my friends would do without me while I was away. Feelings of jealousy stirred inside of me, and the train ride seemed uncomfortable and longer than usual.

Mrs. Hanley was waiting for me on the platform, with Ryan in a stroller, and I was surprised by how much he'd grown. At the house, she asked me to entertain him while she did a few chores. He was able to walk and spoke a few words now, and he seemed as curious about me as I was of him. Mrs. Hanley gave him a bottle when we sat down for tea, and he waddled around the room drinking his milk while we talked about the blizzard. I was startled when he came up behind me and tugged at my clothing. Mrs. Hanley looked pleased.

"He's sweet on ya, Peg. He wants yer attention."

I'd never been around a toddler before and was fascinated by how he communicated his needs. He pulled at people for attention, brought them a book when he wanted to be read to, cried by the kitchen sink when he was hungry, and called "Mam, mam," when he was tired.

Mr. Hanley paid more attention to Ryan now that he was bigger, and spent time playing with him in the evening while Mrs. Hanley and I went for a walk. Before I got into bed, Mrs. Hanley came into the room and stood there looking at me with her hands on her hips.

"Peg, yer gettin so big. I can't believe yer goin ta be ten years old this summer. I guess ya won't be needin me ta lie down with ya anymore."

I just smiled and slid in between the sheets, and then she said good night, kissed my forehead, and left the room. I wanted to cry. I'd loved the feeling of her weight beside me, and inhaling her scent was always so comforting. We didn't celebrate birthdays at the industrial school, but I knew I had to be ten to go into Fifth Class, and I guess that was too old to have someone lying in bed next to you. I lay there thinking about Ryan, and couldn't help but wonder what I'd been like at his age. Who taught me to walk and talk? Did I ever call out "Mam" to my mother? I tried to remember, but nothing came to me, except a feeling of deep sadness.

While walking to town the following day, I tried to teach Ryan different words. When I pointed to a horse pulling a cart on the street, he said, "Orse, orse," and Mrs. Hanley and I clapped with excitement. That was when I decided to teach him to say "Peg."

Mr. Hanley watched as I sat with Ryan after supper, trying to get him to say my name.

"Peg, he's like a puppy, ya've gotta give em somethin ta get a response."

I had nothing to give him, so I made funny faces and clowned around to get his attention, all the while saying "Peg, say Peg."

It was during the third day of my visit when Ryan finally said, "Peg."

I was thrilled, and in an odd way, hearing him say my name made me feel special. I gave him a hug and a kiss, and it was obvious that the Hanleys were very impressed.

Ryan napped every day after lunch for two hours, and during that time, I had Mrs. Hanley all to myself. I'd given up hope of living with them, but I still loved spending time with her, and dreamed about staying with them anyway.

I was glad to see Granny when she came for her mid-week visit, but I'd noticed she kept calling Ryan the wrong name. Mrs. Hanley was very upset by this, and I was taken aback when she snapped at her mam.

"Stop callin him Martin!"

After Granny left, she told me that her mam forgets a lot of things lately.

Mrs. Hanley sat on the bench in Eyre Square watching me walk Ryan around the park. I brought him over to the other children and they thought he was my little brother. One of the girls said he looked just like me, so I pretended to be his big sister.

On our way back to the house, we walked along Forster Street, and I looked down the drive where a large wooden gate, between high stone walls, had been left ajar. There was a building that looked similar to the industrial school and I asked Mrs. Hanley about it.

"Tis a home, but not fer children. The Maggies live there."

"Who are the Maggies?"

"They're women who work doin laundry fer the nuns."

"Is it an industrial school for adults?"

She hesitated before answering me.

"Somethin like that, but they haven't got it as good as ye."

I was disappointed we didn't see Delia and her daughters or go to the beach during this visit, but I still enjoyed myself. We went in to town frequently, and during one of our trips, Mrs. Hanley bought me a red purse, and Mr. Hanley put a shilling into it.

In bed at night, I tried not to entertain thoughts about living with them, but it was a struggle. I wanted to live in this house and be part of this family. I wanted a normal, acceptable life. It would be perfect. I could be the big sister. I could help Mrs. Hanley around the house and watch Ryan. People would think we were really siblings with our matching hair and eyes.

On Sunday morning in mass, I prayed to God, once again asking Him to let me stay. I was surprised at how sad I felt about leaving Ryan. From the window on the train, I waved goodbye and wondered if the little boy would miss me.

When I returned to the industrial school, I hid my new purse under the clothing in my box and hoped the nuns wouldn't take it. As I headed for the yard, Sister Constance stopped me in the hallway. She was giving instructions to a group of girls and told me to help them.

On our way out to the barn, we had to pass the greenhouse, where Mathew Campbell stood in the doorway waving a big, fat, red tomato, trying to get our attention.

"Who wants one? I've got plenty in here fer ya."

I was ready to run over, but one of the girls stopped me.

"Don't ya dare. He just wants ta kiss ya and get in yer hole."

"Huh?"

"He'll be wantin ta touch ya and get in yer pants."

Mr. Campbell was waiting for us with several pails of fresh milk lined up by the barn door. The pails were heavy and I was glad when we stopped for a break after passing the greenhouse. Two girls pulled tin cups out from under their clothes and filled them with the thick, fresh cream that floated to the top of their pails. Then they passed their cups around so each of us could do the same.

"It tastes heavenly!"

"Why don't we get this in our cocoa?"

"The nuns take the cream and give us the watery stuff at the bottom."

When we were done, I looked for Mary and Patsy in the yard, but they were nowhere to be found. At supper they told me that they'd jumped the gate and went into town again. Mary boasted about the good time they had.

"We were running all over town and now I'm starvin."

"Well, I'm not that hungry because I had globs of cream today! Tis a shame ya missed it."

∞

The following day, after completing our jobs, Sister Constance doled out extra assignments. Mary and I were sent to the creamery to help Sister Bernadette make butter. Fortunately, for me, Patsy was sent to clean the dorms, and I would have time alone with Mary. I mentioned my surprise that she'd taken such a risk going to town while Sister Constance was here; it was very unlike her. She didn't respond. When we passed the greenhouse, I warned her about Mathew Campbell. Up ahead I could see Sister Bernadette waiting for us outside the creamery, a small stone building by the barn.

Over the next few days, we churned gallons of milk into butter, paddled it, and then poured it into crocks and molds. It was hard work, and Sister Bernadette's presence kept us from having a private conversation, but at least we were spending time together, without Patsy. The only time we were alone was when we had to haul wagons loaded with butter up to the convent. We'd stop after passing the greenhouse and pop a few pats into our mouths, savoring the rich, salty butter. I felt like this time together brought us closer again—so when we went to confession at Saint Michael's on Saturday I was upset that she partnered with Patsy. I fell into line behind them with Erin. As the line of girls snaked through town, I watched the two of them ahead of me talking and laughing. When we turned onto Market Street, Erin nudged me and pointed up the hill toward Saint Grellan's Terrace, a government housing development for poor families.

"C'mon, let's go see my mam."

Without thinking, I joined her running up the hill and through the maze of tiny houses. Her mother, a large, somber-looking woman, was sitting on a chair outside her front door. She struggled to her feet and gave Erin a big hug and a kiss. Then she turned toward me.

"And who've we got here?"

"This is Peg. She works with me in the convent."

"Ah, she's just a wee bit of thing. What can she do?"

"We've all gotta do jobs, Mam."

"I know, I know. God bless those Mercys. I know they're not the most maternal women, but without em, many of ye wouldn't have a roof over yer head or food in yer belly."

Our visit was short, and we raced back down the hill and into Saint Michael's Square. Before entering the church, I asked Erin why she didn't live with her mam.

"No money," said Erin. "Pa is in the asylum and my brothers took off ta America."

Mary was looking toward the door as we slipped inside and took a seat in the pew behind her.

In September I was assigned to work in the convent kitchen helping Sister Rita. Mary was assigned to clean the sacristy behind the chapel, which happened to be right over the convent kitchen. She would call out my name, and I'd go to the window and look up to see her waving down at me. Sometimes when we walked back to the industrial school, I'd share the butter sandwich Sister Rita gave me each morning. When classes started, I began to hide the sandwich in the boiler room and eat it later in the day.

Erin came into the kitchen daily to get breakfast for Father Doherty, which he ate in the parlor after saying morning mass. We'd chat a bit while Sister Rita loaded his tray.

"Erin, yer so lucky ta be workin in the china press."

"I am. I can only hope I'll be as lucky when Mother Bernard gives me my situation. I'll die if she sends me ta Dublin or Galway! I've got ta stay close ta home ta check on my mam."

"I don't know where I'd like ta go fer my situation, but I know I don't want ta stay in Ballinasloe."

"Well, ya've got a few more years."

∞

Sister Anthony, our Fifth Class teacher, told us about the starving children in Africa. She held up a plastic figurine of brown child wearing a red vest sitting on a box. We watched as she put a penny in the figure's mechanical hand, which triggered it to rise and deposit the coin in its mouth.

"For each penny you donate, I'll give you a black strap."

Mary and I watched with envy as a few of the town's children made their donation and then unraveled the long string of black licorice rolled into a pinwheel that they received for their good deed. Mary urged me to donate some of the money I'd gotten from Granny, but I said no.

∞

When the season changed and the cold weather arrived, we'd race over to the convent each morning and stop for a few minutes by the heater inside the rear convent door. It was unusual to see the kitchen door ajar.

"Looks like Sister Rita burned somethin."

"It still smells good, whatever it is!"

"She's a good cook, sometimes she lets me taste things."

"Is she still givin ya butter sandwiches?"

"Yes, but I eat em before I leave the kitchen. Someone found my hiding spot and has been takin em."

As I entered the kitchen, Sister Rita was about to step out, with a brown bag in her hand.

"I'll be back soon, Peg. I've got ta toss this burnt bit and then I'm goin ta talk ta Mother Bernard."

I cracked open the kitchen window and saw Sister Rita toss the bag into trash bin. As I filled my bucket with water, a commotion outside the window caught my attention. I looked out again, and saw Mary rifling through the trash bin and pulling out the brown bag. I watched her pop the charred bits of meat into her mouth.

Later that day, I asked her about it.

"How long have ya been takin food from the trash bins?"

"Since I'm workin in the sacristy. Sometimes I'll find a few half-eaten buns, and they're good as new. They're a lot better than porridge."

I couldn't believe she hadn't told me about this, and then it dawned on me.

"Mary, do they taste better than a butter sandwich?"

CHAPTER EIGHT

It was a Saturday morning and I'd just finished cleaning the tables when Mother Bernard appeared at the kitchen door.

"You've got a letter, Peg," she said, handing me a white envelope.

I tucked it in my waistband and ran back to the industrial school and into one of the toilet stalls for privacy. It was the first piece of mail I'd ever received.

The front of the envelope read, *Mary Margaret Joyce c/o Saint Thomas Industrial School, Society Street, Ballinasloe, Ireland*, with a green postage stamp in the upper right corner. On the back flap was Mrs. Hanley's name and address. The envelope had already been opened. I carefully removed the Christmas card and opened it. A shilling was taped above a short note.

December 17, 1947
Dear Peg,

We are thinking of you during this Christmas Holiday and wishing you well. Hopefully, we will have a better winter than last year.

The new year will be bringing us an addition to the family, as we are expecting another child. Ryan is growing like a weed and he doesn't seem like a baby anymore. He's become quite a hand full, with lots of energy and the gift of the gab, much like his father.

Granny recently hurt her back. The doctor has given her tablets for pain, but she doesn't always remember to take them. Please put her in your prayers.

We are looking forward to seeing you again next summer.

Love, Norah Hanley

I rubbed the shilling between my fingers and reread the card several times before putting it back in the envelope. The news of a new baby was upsetting. I'd carried hope since the summer that Mr. and Mrs. Hanley might like to have a sister for Ryan, and that could be me. Another baby would take up more space in the house and more of Mrs. Hanley's time and attention.

My distress was obvious, and Mary asked me what was wrong. I handed her the card, which she read and then gave to Patsy. Patsy read the card and then asked me if Norah Hanley was my relation.

"No, I just visit her in the summer. I don't have any relations."

"Well, ya gotta have relations! Ya didn't come from nowhere, at the very least ya've gotta have a mam! And look, she signed it *love*. That means somethin."

⚬∞⚬

That night Patsy's words replayed over and over in my mind. I guess I never wanted to think about it. It was easier to accept that I was alone, without family. The truth was, I wanted to have family. Even if my mam had died or was in a hospital or an asylum, I had to have other relations. Why wouldn't they come for me? As I cried myself to sleep I quickly realized why I avoided thinking about it.

I wasn't aware Sister Rita was watching me as I scrubbed the tables in the nuns' refectory.

"Peg, is somethin at ya?"

I put my rag down, sat in one of the chairs, and began to cry. She came over and sat down beside me.

"Peg, tell me dear, what's botherin ya?"

I sat for a few minutes, debating whether or not to ask her. Finally, I wiped my eyes and took a deep breath.

"Sister Rita, do ya know who my mam is?"

She sighed and patted my head.

"Ah Peg, I'm so sorry. Yer an illegitimate, ya've got no family."

"But I still have ta have a mam."

"Well yes, that's true, but it's not the same. Ya were born from an act of sin."

"Sin? Am I goin ta hell?"

"Oh Peg, when yer born out of wedlock, ya've got no family. But don't ya worry yerself, Peg, the Lord is very forgivin."

Mary, Patsy, and I huddled together in the yard, trying to generate some heat.

"I asked Sister Rita about my mam. She says I'm an illegitimate."

Mary gasped. "What are ya, an egit? Ya don't ask a nun a question like that!"

Patsy nodded. "My mam used ta say all the girls in the industrial schools are orphans. I don't think yer supposed ta say yer an illegitimate because people'll be looking down on ya."

The desire to know my roots was building, even if I was an illegitimate. I had to have relations of some kind and began to wonder if I
had a connection with the Clearys. I hoped I didn't. The Clearys were
not nice people.

Surely Mrs. Cleary knew who my family was, and may have told
Mrs. Hanley. I'd asked Mrs. Hanley once, but she said she didn't
know. Would she lie to me?

Over the next few months I obsessed about my mother, the
woman who named me Mary Margaret Joyce. I tried to recall my
past, but my memories were vague. My encounters with people other
than the Clearys were rare. I didn't attend Infants Class in school or
go to church, and the only visitors were a neighbor, Mr. Lally, and
Mrs. Hanley. I recall Mrs. Hanley being very kind to me during her
visits. She'd bring me little gifts of sweets or hair clips. As I muddled
over my memories, I was unsure if they were accurate or fantasy; but
I couldn't help but feel Mrs. Hanley may have a connection to me. It
was as if she'd been keeping tabs on me. Could I be her daughter? No,
she has a family. Surely, she'd take me in if I was her daughter.

In July, I sat on the train thinking of ways to bring up the subject
about my mam and any relations I might have during my visit. Mary
and Patsy advised me not to bring it up, especially since I was an
illegitimate. Mary also warned me that if Sister Constance found out,
I'd get a whippin.

Mrs. Hanley was waiting for me at the station. Ryan stood beside
the pram where his new baby sister, Rachel, slept soundly. Rachel was
beautiful. She looked like a doll, and now the Hanleys had a daughter.

I smiled and told Mrs. Hanley she was lovely, but inside I felt sad they had a little girl. I wanted to be their daughter.

At the house, Ryan clamored for my attention, and I took him into the yard so he wouldn't wake the baby. During supper, Mrs. Hanley told me she appreciated that I looked after Ryan all afternoon. He was a handful, and I was exhausted. Thankfully Mr. Hanley paid him lots of attention after supper. I cleared the plates and scrubbed the pots, so Mrs. Hanley could tend to Rachel.

Since Rachel slept in the pram, Ryan shared the bed with me. He even moved in his sleep, twisting and turning, but I was so tired that I fell asleep quickly anyway. In the morning, I eased out of bed, trying not to wake him. I offered to make the bread while Mrs. Hanley cooked the porridge. She glanced over at me while I kneaded the dough and said I was doing a very good job.

Delia came over for a visit later in the day, and I was disappointed her girls weren't with her. Mrs. Hanley invited me to join them for tea, but after I sat down, Ryan ran circles around the table. I drank and ate quickly and then took him out to the yard, so they could have a peaceful visit.

That evening Mrs. Hanley told me her sister, Hannah, and her two sons were here in Ireland for a few weeks. They were staying with Granny, and would be in for a visit with her on Wednesday.

I was feeding Rachel a bottle when Granny came into the house, and a modern-looking woman carrying two large shopping bags walked in behind her. As Mrs. Hanley embraced her sister, two boys, not much bigger than Ryan, barreled into the kitchen and almost knocked over the pram. Before Mrs. Hanley could greet them, they grabbed Ryan and ran out into the yard. Mrs. Hanley took Rachel from my arms for her sister to admire and then placed her back in the pram.

I sat quietly in the green chair watching the stylish American woman unpack her bags. She was placing canisters of tea and containers of dry fruit on the table when I caught her attention and she gasped.

"Mary Margaret?"

"It's Peg," Mrs. Hanley quickly cut in. "Peg, this is my sister, Hannah."

I stood up and walked over to the table and extended my hand. Hannah grabbed me and hugged me tightly. Then took a step back and looked at me, scanning me from head to toe, making me feel very self-conscious. The awkward feeling was disrupted as the three boys came racing back into the house. The commotion made Mrs. Hanley nervous, but it didn't seem to faze her sister. Granny took control and ordered them back out to the yard, and then she began to rock the pram to settle Rachel.

I sat at the table with the women drinking tea, quietly listening to their conversation. Hannah gave me two lovely frocks that buttoned down the front—she called them shirtwaist dresses. As I stood and held one of the dresses against me, I realized Hannah was the woman who'd sent me new outfits every year. Hannah asked me several questions about my classes and Mrs. Hanley sat quietly listening to my answers. When Hannah asked me about the industrial school I lived in, Mrs. Hanley interrupted before I could respond.

"Peg, would ya please go outside and mind the boys."

I was relieved because it felt awkward talking about the industrial school to other people. I sat on the back step and watched as the boys ran wild about the yard. Hannah appeared at the back door with a plate of buttered slices of bread.

"Fer the boys," she said as she handed me the plate.

"I helped Mrs. Hanley make the bread this mornin."

"It's lovely, I just ate a slice. Ya did a fine job."

Granny appeared behind her, pushing open the rear door.

"Hannah, I've got ta get back. Are ya ready ta go?"

"What's yer rush?"

"I've got ta bring Father Cosgrove some eggs."

"Mam, don't ya remember? We stopped ta see him on the way inta town!"

They both went back inside and I took the bread over to the boys. The Americans were chattering away and I could see Ryan had trouble understanding their accents. Their visit lasted until late in the afternoon, and it was obvious Mrs. Hanley was relieved when they left. She was very quiet that evening and appeared to be distressed about something. I'd expected her to be filled with happiness after a visit with her sister.

∞

The following morning during breakfast, Mrs. Hanley told me that Hannah needed my help with some shopping she had to do.

"I'd be happy ta help her."

"Ya don't have ta go."

"Oh no, I'd like ta go."

I gobbled down my breakfast and dressed in one of the new frocks. Then I brushed my hair the best I could, trying to flatten it down. To my surprise, Hannah arrived without her sons. I thought she needed my help to watch over the boys. Instead, I'd be spending time alone with her, something I'd hardly been able to do with Mrs. Hanley during this trip.

Hannah didn't dress like anyone from Galway. She wore a bright, lime-green blouse with a gold pin on the collar. Her skirt, shoes, and handbag were all the same cream color, and her hair was twisted up behind her head and secured with an expensive-looking clip.

I looked at her admiringly.

Mrs. Hanley rolled her eyes. "Would ya look at the style of her!" she said, somewhat sarcastically.

As we left the house, Mrs. Hanley called out behind us, "Mind the time, I'll be needin Peg back ta help me."

Hannah walked at a quick pace and I moved as fast as I could to keep up with her. She drilled me with questions about the industrial school, asking me what we ate, where we slept, and what we did each day. In town she went in and out of all the shoppes, looking at linens and dishes. She made a large purchase and told the shop owner to ship them to her house in America.

"Peg, there's nothin like Irish linens and china."

We walked through Eyre Square and she looked at her watch. "It's time fer tea. Let's go ta the Great Southern."

I could feel my heart pounding as we walked up the marble steps into the grand hotel. I felt awkward in the elegant lobby, where we were greeted by a man in a perfectly pressed blue uniform and white gloves.

"I'd like a table in the Oyster Grill Restaurant fer my niece and I," she said.

Stunned by her words, I stood there speechless.

"Come on, Peg," she said, as she headed toward the staircase we'd been directed to.

I followed her down the steps and into the restaurant, where a young lady wearing a crisp white blouse and black skirt led us to a table. Hannah ordered for us and then placed the cloth napkin on her lap before returning her attention to me.

"Peg, is somethin wrong?"

"I heard ya say, I was yer niece. Are ya my relation?"

She hesitated only for a second before responding.

"Well sure, Peg, yer like family. Aren't we all related in Ireland? I want ya ta call me Auntie Hannah."

"Do ya know my family?"

A waitress appeared before she could answer me and poured our tea, leaving the china pot on the table. Hannah never answered my question, quickly changing the topic.

"I'm famished," she said.

The waitress reappeared with a three-tiered platter filled with an assortment of scones and buns, two types of jam, and pats of fresh butter. While we ate, Hannah talked about how wonderful it was to live in America. I had trouble paying attention because I kept thinking about her comment, "My niece."

"There's opportunity fer everyone in America. Especially if yer educated and a hard worker. It's a mass mix of people, culture, and high energy."

"It sounds like an exciting place ta live."

"There's loads of Irish and the clubs have grand dances fer the young ones ta meet up. Maybe when yer done with Secondary School ya'll come out."

"None of the girls go ta Secondary School."

Hannah put down her cup and tilted her head thoughtfully, and then repeated my words.

"None of the girls go ta Secondary School?"

"Not that I know of. We go ta Sixth Class, then work in the industrial school until we're placed in a situation at the age of fifteen."

There was an awkward silence, and I felt as if I'd said something wrong.

"Well Peg, if yer ta come ta America, ya need an education."

"We've got one more stop," Hannah said as we left the hotel. I walked alongside of her until she stopped at a hair salon and opened the door. Inside a fashionable woman sat at the front counter.

Hannah pointed to my hair and looked at the woman.

"Can ya tame this mane?"

"We sure can."

Hannah took a seat on a sofa by the counter and the woman took me to a chair, wrapped a cape around my neck, and tilted my head back toward a sink and washed my hair. Then she took me over to a chair in front of a large mirror. I had a full view of myself and smiled as I looked into my own bright blue eyes. For the first time I noticed how fair my skin was and that my nose was turned up at the tip. I gasped as the first snip of the shears sent a clump of my thick curly blond hair to the floor. When the woman was done, I had a short, curly bob that barely reached my shoulders. I smiled at the girl in the mirror. She looked pretty and fashionable. Slowly, I turned my head to the left and then to the right, trying to get a complete view. When I jerked my head back to the center, my soft, smooth hair fell perfectly into place. I felt like a different person and held my shoulders back and head high as we walked back to the house.

Hannah was quite pleased with my new look. Mrs. Hanley was not. She was stunned when we walked into the house and immediately sent me outside with Ryan. I stood by the back door, trying to hear the sisters argue. Mrs. Hanley said Hannah had no rights over me and it wasn't her place to have my hair cut. Ryan kept trying to get my attention, making it difficult for me to listen. I heard Hannah call Mrs. Hanley selfish and then she appeared at the rear door and stepped outside. I could hear Mrs. Hanley crying inside. Hannah said goodbye to Ryan and then hugged me tightly.

"Do yerself a favor, Peg. Learn all ya can and get out of Ireland. There's nothin here fer ya."

The rest of my visit was terribly awkward. Mrs. Hanley didn't say much and I spent most of my time playing with Ryan while she tended to her new baby girl. Granny stopped in on Saturday and gave me a sixpence.

"Thanks, Granny. I'll put it with the others in my red purse."

"Ya mean, ya haven't spent em?"

"Nope, I'm savin them."

She nodded, looking very pleased. "Well, that's good. Savin money is important."

I gave her a hug and said goodbye.

Sunday morning after mass, Hannah came to the house and gave me a gift of a handsome plaid satchel. "For yer trip ta America someday," she said, with a wink.

CHAPTER NINE

When my train arrived in Ballinasloe, I ran back to the industrial school to show off my new hair style. I could see the heads turn and hear the whispers of the other girls as I stepped into the yard.

"It looked better long," said Mary.

"I like it," said Patsy, "ya look older."

"Well, the hairdresser said it's the latest style," I told them.

As we stood there chatting, I realized the other girls were eyeing my satchel, too, and I needed to put it away. On my way to the dorm, I looked down the corridor and, for the first time, really noticed how bleak this place was. I felt myself beginning to build a resentment. Why should I have to live here?

I encountered Sister Constance in the hallway. She looked me over scornfully from head to toe. After a few curt comments about my new hairstyle and fashionable satchel, she reassigned me to work in the laundry.

In the dorm, I slid the satchel under my bed and exhaled a sigh of relief, feeling oddly grateful that my punishment was just to work a harder job.

The following morning, I took a deep breath before entering the laundry, where I'd be working with girls who had a reputation for being "pissin mad!" Julia sent me over to the nun in charge, who assigned me to sort the clean, folded clothes by number. When I was done, she sent me over to help Angela.

"Well, aren't ya turnin inta quite a looker!" said Angela, and then she motioned for me to grab the handle of a large wicker basket.

We hauled the heavy load of wet sheets out to the clotheslines by the orchard.

"Ya can be sure they're watchin the clock on us," she said, swiftly moving down the line, hanging one sheet after another.

On the way back, Angela waved to a girl who was laying small white rags out on the grass in the adjacent field. I asked her what the girl was doing and she said, "That's where ya dry yer rags for yer monthly."

I nodded, but had no idea what she was talking about.

Working in the laundry that summer proved to be quite an education. The girls cursed, smoked, talked back to the nuns, and spoke freely about their scandalous liaisons with the Garbally boys in town. They were a tough group, but I saw their soft side when they sang together to pass the long, hot work day.

In mid-August, Sister Constance relieved me of my penance, and reassigned me to polishing the pews in the convent chapel. On my

way to the chapel each morning, I'd catch a glimpse of the renova-
tions being made to add a new dormitory on the first floor in the
convent. The dormitory would accommodate a dozen out-of-town
students attending the Sisters of Mercy's Secondary School. Very few
of the locals could afford the tuition to send their daughters and they
needed to increase their enrollment.

In September, a large round table was put in the industrial school
refectory where the new boarders would have their meals. Their
meals were prepared and served by Sister Simone, who was known
to be a wonderful cook. My mouth watered each morning when she
passed our table carrying trays of freshly baked buns.

The boarders were dressed in smart navy-blue pinafores over
starched white blouses, with blue neck ties. Pretty ribbons and clips
kept their well-groomed hair in place. Their voices sounded airy and
light and they often giggled with each other while they sat at their
table eating. I envied this group of girls that stood out so vividly in
this dreary environment, and wondered what they thought of me, of
us, the house children.

Sixth Class, our last year of formal education, was taught by Sister
Eucharia, and listening to her daily lectures was brutal. The old,
wrinkled nun waved a finger from her trembling hand as she warned
us about sin and the evils lurking in the world. I spent most of my
time in her class daydreaming, either about the times I'd spent in
Galway or what the future held for me. Frequently, I reflected on the
words of advice from Hannah, "There's opportunity fer everyone in
America. Especially if yer educated and a hard worker. Learn all ya

can, and get out of Ireland." And that's when my desire to travel to America began to grow.

At the end of the school year we'd have to work for the nuns until we were sent out for our situation. Mary and I would often pass the time, anticipating where we'd eventually wind up working.

"I heard they're sendin lots a girls ta Dublin, fer cleanin in the hospital," said Mary.

"Ugh! I don't want ta be cleanin fer people."

"Maybe she'll send ya ta a family ta care fer their children."

"I don't want ta do that either!"

"Well, unless ya can cook, I don't know what else there is!"

"Maybe I'll go to the States."

Mary rolled her eyes, dismissing me and my "grand ideas!"

After the nuns left for their conference in Dublin, the sky opened and the rain came down in buckets, disrupting our plans for the brisk, cool October afternoon. Instead of jumping the gate, we went inside to find a place to sit among the chaos. Younger girls screamed as they raced up and down the hallways, while the older girls argued and fought in the rec room. Katie and Julia yelled threats at everyone in an attempt to gain order.

Mary, Patsy, and I escaped the madness up in the dorms, pushing two beds together and lying across them, where we could talk. Just as we were getting comfortable, Theresa came running into the room.

"Hey Patsy," she said, "ya better get down ta the rec room. They're beatin on yer sister, Grace."

Patsy jumped up and ran downstairs, and Theresa lay down in the vacant spot beside us. She pulled her knees up to her stomach and let out a little moan.

"What's wrong with ya?" Mary asked.

"Ugh, I'm bleedin!" Theresa said, "It's the cramps, ya know."

Our reaction told Theresa we were clueless.

"It's yer monthly, when ya bleed from yer private parts."

"Disgustin!" yelled Mary, pulling a pillow over her head.

"How do ya stop it?" I asked.

"Ya can't. Ya stuff white rags in yer knickers, so it's not dripping down yer legs. If the nuns see ya bleeding through yer clothes, ya'll get a thrashin!"

Theresa continued giving us the details of adolescent development. She said we'd grow pubic hair and that our bosoms would grow.

"Some of the girls wrap rags around their chests ta try and stop em from getting bigger. But I don't think that works."

Theresa said it usually happens in the Sixth Class and then warned us, "Beware of Sister Agnes in the washroom. She'll be snappin the towel off ya ta get a look. I think she's queer."

We began to check our bodies daily for changes.

※

In November, I received my second piece of mail. Mother Bernard handed me a light blue envelope. "From America," she said with a smile. I looked at the return address on the back flap before tucking it in my waistband. It was from Aunt Hannah. I went straight to the toilet and took the letter out of the already opened envelope. An American five-dollar bill was in the folded sheet of writing paper.

November 18, 1948

Dear Peg,

It was a delight spending time with you in Galway. You've turned into quite a young lady. I hope you've been able to maintain your new hairstyle, it makes you look so refined.

I know Norah enjoys your visits with her each summer.

She has her hands full with the two little ones, and I can see that you're a big help to her.

My boys had such a great time that they can't wait to go back. I think they are farm boys at heart.

I hope you are doing well in the Sixth Class. Maybe the Good Lord will see to it that you go to Secondary School. Always remember, education is your key to a better life.

I'm enclosing some money for you to buy yourself something special.

God bless,

Auntie Hannah

As I reread the letter someone started banging on the stall door. There were only two toilets, and the other was broken, but I didn't care. I turned the money over in my hand, and read the letter a third time. I wouldn't tell anyone about it, not even Mary. I went upstairs and hid the letter and the money in my red purse.

I couldn't pay attention to Sister Eucharia that day thinking about the five-dollar bill, but then she started banging her ruler on the desk.

"A former inmate of the industrial school, Rebecca Murphy, is entering a marriage today with a Protestant. Let us take this moment and pray for her."

We bowed our heads and clasped our hands to pray for the Catholic girl, Rebecca Murphy, about to marry a Protestant boy.

"May the Lord have mercy on her."

At the end of the day, Sister Eucharia told me to stay behind after class with Patsy and a girl named Clare. I didn't know Clare well. The other house children made fun of her because she walked around with a book tucked under her arm all the time. The three of us sat looking at each other while Sister Eucharia dismissed the town's children. When the classroom was empty she came over to us.

"You'll be taking an exam this Saturday at ten o'clock. The exam is on mathematics and reading comprehension."

She dismissed us without further explanation, and we didn't ask any questions—we'd been trained never to question the nuns.

"I wonder what that's all about," I said as we left the Primary School.

"Secondary School admission," said Clare.

"How do ya know that?" asked Patsy.

"My pa sent me a letter. He said Mother Bernard said I can attend Secondary School if I pass the examination and he can pay my tuition."

"Ya may be right," said Patsy. "My aunt paid fer my sister Margy ta go ta nursin school after she found out she was washin the floors in the rectory. Maybe she spoke ta Mother Bernard about sending me ta Secondary School so I don't have ta be a skivvy when I leave here."

I knew if Clare was right, then there was a big mistake. There was no one to pay my tuition.

On Saturday morning, the three of us took the exam with a dozen other girls. The proctor, a plain-looking man with a bald head and rather pale skin, read from an attendance sheet, "Mary Margaret Joyce."

I wasn't used to being called by my given name, and I hesitated for a moment before raising my hand.

He distributed the test, and then set a timer. Two hours later, he collected our papers and told us the exams would be graded in Dublin and the results would sent by mail at the end of January.

It was a few days before Christmas. I was on my way to the convent chapel when Erin stopped me outside of the china press.

"Mother Bernard wants ta see ya in her office when yer done."

I quickly polished the pews and rushed over to her office. Sister Xavier was seated just outside of the office and pointed to the door as I approached.

"Go on in, Mother Bernard is waiting for you."

I pushed the hair out of my face and patted down my clothing before gently turning the knob on the heavy door. Mother Bernard was sitting in a high-back chair behind a large wooden desk. On her desk was a black telephone, a neat pile of papers, a ledger, and a small brown box. Behind her was a highly polished credenza filled with books and one small framed photograph of two young girls.

"A parcel arrived for you," she said, sliding the box across her desk toward me.

I glanced down at the box and then back at her. She nodded, "Go ahead, take it."

"What'd she want?" Erin called to me as I rushed pass the china press toward the corridor leading to the back door.

"I got a package!" I said excitedly, holding up the box.

I stood against the wall, with the box behind my back, waiting for one of the bathroom stalls to be free. Finally, in private, I removed the contents—a stack of light blue writing paper, matching envelopes, and a Christmas card. I opened the card. It held another American five-dollar bill.

December 5, 1948

Dear Peg,

The weather has been dreadfully cold here. We don't have the dampness you have in Ireland, but we do have lots of snow and freezing temperatures. The boys love to play outside building snowmen and sleigh riding, I've got a job to get them back in the house.

The holiday season is upon us and we are all very excited. This year my brother Martin and his new wife, along with my sister Margaret, her husband James and their son Connor will be coming to celebrate Christmas Day with us. It'll be grand to have them here, but I do miss Granny and Norah terribly during the holidays.

Please let me know how you fared on the entrance exams. I've enclosed some money for you to buy stamps and look forward to hearing from you soon.

Have a Merry Christmas,
God Bless,
Auntie Hannah

And so I learned who would fund my secondary education, if I passed the exam. I couldn't keep the news to myself and ran to the yard to find Mary and Patsy.

"Maybe she's yer mam!" said Patsy.

"That'd make sense," said Mary. "Why else would she be sendin that money?"

Suddenly, I wished that I hadn't mentioned it to them.

I couldn't fall asleep that night, wondering if Hannah could be my mam. Did she leave me behind so she could go to America? Is it guilt that made her send me clothes every summer? Was Norah Hanley keeping tabs on me for her sister?

I cried myself to sleep that night, and every other night through the Christmas holiday. I didn't write to Hannah as she'd asked me to.

At the end of January, Clare, Patsy, and I were called to Mother Bernard's office. The frosty morning air bit at our skin as we ran over to the convent. Nervously, we sat in the brocade-covered chairs in front of her desk while she reviewed papers Sister Xavier handed to her. I noticed the frame on her credenza had been moved and I wondered who the two girls in the photograph were.

Mother Bernard put down the papers, folded her hands in front of her and smiled.

"You've passed the entrance examination, and the three of you will be attending Scoil Mhuire Secondary School in September."

CHAPTER TEN

Sister Eucharia wore us down with prayers for our salvation, and the end of the school year couldn't come quick enough for me. Even the drudgery of the yard looked inviting after listening to her lectures about chastity and the evil temptations that we would be challenged by.

While Patsy and I stood in line to trade in our shoes for summer sandals, we talked about the changes we'd noticed in Mary. Mary was grieving her sister's departure to Dublin; she'd been sent there for her situation, cleaning at Saint Vincent's Hospital. She was isolating, frequently sneaking off on her own. I knew it also pained her that Patsy and I were admitted to Secondary School and she was not even offered the opportunity.

Later, in the yard, Patsy fretted about being alone during my trip to Galway. She was considered something of an outcast in the industrial school, and hardly had any friends. It had been especially difficult for her, since she'd been one of the town's children until she was ten, when her mother died. I couldn't imagine how awful it must be for her. It was a struggle for me to adjust after returning from just one week of a normal life in Galway. I hated readjusting to the restrictions of our routine, the institutional food, and most of all, the lack of individuality. Life at the industrial school could be depressing, especially after experiencing the alternative. Neither of my two best friends were happy, and there was nothing I could do to help them.

On my way to the train station I saw Mary sitting with a boy in the green. I waved, but she ignored me.

"She's lookin fer trouble!" said one of the girls I was walking with.

I nodded in agreement, feeling concerned about my dear friend. Seeing her confirmed the rumors I'd heard about her jumping the gate to hang around with boys.

I boarded the train and carefully placed my satchel on the overhead shelf and settled into my seat. I watched with envy as a mother and daughter interacted in the seat ahead of me. The mother adjusted the girl's hair clips, and spoke softly to her, as if sharing a secret. I closed my eyes and visualized myself sitting with my own mother, talking and laughing. My mother would look down at me and smile, and in my mind, my mother had Hannah's face. The tears welled up in my eyes, and I turned my head to look out of the window as I tried to dismiss the thought. I conjured up the image of myself dressed in a Secondary School uniform, attending classes and socializing with my classmates. My fear of rejection and being taunted by the girls of privilege emerged in my daydream, so I pushed all my thoughts out of my mind and simply tried to take in the view of the passing farms and towns.

Norah Hanley looked unsettled, standing on the platform with one hand bracing Rachel's stroller and the other pulling at a fidgeting Ryan by her side. When we arrived at the house, she collapsed into the chair and stated she was exhausted and that the heat was getting to her. I saw her eye my satchel as I set it down on the floor, and I immediately felt uncomfortable. I wondered if the satchel was a reminder of how Hannah had fussed over me. In an odd way, I felt like a pawn the two sisters struggled to take control of.

I set the table, put the kettle on the burner, and gave Rachel a bottle. Ryan impatiently waited while I buttered a slice of bread for him before sending him out to the yard. All the while, Norah sat watching me from the chair.

"Oh Peg, you're a godsend," she said as I poured the tea.

I felt relieved that she seemed pleased with me when she sat down at the table. Then I told her my big news—that I'd passed the entrance exam for Secondary School. She appeared stunned and clearly knew nothing about it. I didn't mention Hannah's letters, realizing that, for some reason, Hannah chose not to tell her.

During the first few days of my visit, I found myself working harder than I did at the industrial school. If I wasn't doing household chores, I was watching Ryan and Rachel; but I was happy to help Norah because it made me feel needed and like part of their family. During supper, Dan asked Ryan to pick a horse in the upcoming races, and it triggered a memory of how I'd felt before the Hanleys had their own children. I recall arriving each year with the hope of never having to leave. They doted on me, making me feel special, making me feel wanted. After they had Ryan, I felt abandoned by them, and when they had Rachel, I began to lose all hope of being asked to stay. It had been my great desire to be their child, part of their family, and truthfully, that desire still remains deep within.

On Wednesday morning, while I was making the bread, Norah told me her sister Margaret would be coming for tea with her husband and son. They were visiting from America and staying at a house in Salt Hill. I recalled Hannah mentioning them to me in her Christmas card and I was curious to meet them. I was setting the table when they arrived and was very surprised to see a handsome teenaged boy trail in behind his parents.

Connor was especially friendly toward me and I enjoyed the attention. When Norah sent me out to watch Ryan and Rachel in the yard, he came along to keep me company. We talked easily and he told me all about his plans to join the United States Air Force. I told him I had an American stamp with a plane on it and he asked me if I was a stamp collector. In an effort to impress him, I said I was. He raised his eyebrows and said, "How interesting!"

His comment left me without words so I smiled.

"I'll send you some stamps for your collection," he said.

"That would be nice."

"There isn't much I wouldn't do for a pretty girl like you, Peg."

The blood rushed to my head and I looked down at the ground, I didn't know what to say.

Connor's American accent made him sound so worldly, and I hung on to his every word. Thankfully he liked to talk, because I was too nervous and unsure of what to say. Before he left he winked at me and said, "I'll see ya soon."

I went to bed thinking about the handsome American boy I'd become smitten with. Thoughts of him made my stomach feel like it was swirling, but not sickly. It was a new, uneasy, but welcoming feeling.

The following day I was disappointed when Margaret arrived alone. She said Connor went to Moycullen with his pa to help Granny on the farm.

While Margaret and Norah drank tea, I noticed they seemed to have more in common with each other than with Hannah. They even looked alike; they were both pretty, but not fashionable like their younger sister. Margaret spent the whole day with us, doing many of the chores around the house to give Norah a bit of rest. She also spent time doting on Ryan and Rachel, and I imagined she must have been a loving mother to Connor. When I shared that thought with Norah, she told me Connor had been adopted.

"He was a Pan Am baby. Margaret paid a high price ta the Bon Secours ta have him sent ta America," said Norah. "Adoption isn't legal here ya know."

"Wow, he was lucky!"

Norah looked annoyed by my exclamation.

⚭

On Saturday morning I took extra time grooming myself. I wanted to look my best, since Norah said Connor was helping Granny at the market and they would be meeting Margaret here afterwards. Margaret arrived early and invited me to sit with her and Norah while they had tea. I told her about my admission to Secondary School and she was impressed. In Ireland, most children only went to Primary School from ages four to twelve. Secondary education was considered a privilege, reserved for those who could afford it.

I asked her how she felt about Connor going to the Air Force when he completed school, and she said she hoped he'd change his mind and attend Fordham College where they lived in the Bronx, New York. She said she didn't like the idea of him being up in the air.

Ryan and Rachel came to the table looking for Margaret's

attention, and she got up and chased them before scooping them up one at a time and kissing them until they screamed. Norah rolled her eyes and said, "She dotes too much. She'll be lost when Connor leaves."

Granny came into the house with Connor strolling in behind her, carrying two baskets full of produce. He set the baskets on the table and Granny patted him on the head like he was a little boy. "Thanks, Colin."

"Granny, I'm Connor, not Colin."

"Connor, of course," she said, and sat down at the table and looked toward me. "I hear yer doin well in school."

"I am, Granny. I'll be startin Secondary School in September."

"Well, that's grand! But don't forget yer basics."

Connor and I went out to the yard to keep an eye on Ryan and Rachel. We sat on the back step and I asked him what it was like living in America. He told me it was very different from Ireland.

"Peg, I think you'd love it. You should make a trip over and see for yourself."

"I'd love to."

"Well, if you come soon enough, I'll still be there to show you around."

Granny came to the back door to say goodbye and gave us each a sixpence before leaving. Connor put the coin in his pocket, and I told him I wanted to put it in my purse so I wouldn't lose it.

"Go on," he said, then nodded toward Ryan and Rachel. "I'll keep an eye on them."

While I was in the bedroom I could hear Norah and Margaret talking.

"I'd love ta take Peg back with me," said Margaret.

"Well ya can't. It's out of the question," said Norah.

"Yer so selfish, Norah!"

"It looks like Hannah's sendin her ta Secondary School. She's got ta stay in Ireland."

I sat on the bed stunned, feeling more confused than ever. Margaret wanted to take me to the States and Norah said no. I couldn't believe Norah felt she had the authority to speak for me and use Hannah's gift of Secondary School as a reason for me not to go. She didn't even seem happy for me when I told her I'd been admitted. I became more baffled by the interest these three sisters showed in me, and I was sure of my belief that I belonged to them in some way. The thought of being kin to them angered me, because if that were true, then one of them should have taken me into their home. I knew Margaret couldn't have children. Norah seemed to be around for as long as I could remember. She must be my mother . . . unless it's Hannah and she chose to go to America instead of caring for me.

I didn't know what to do, and I couldn't let them know I was listening. I tiptoed out of the bedroom to the back door. I sat down beside Connor and began to cry, and he reached over and stroked my hair. "What's the matter ,Peg?"

"Connor, please tell me. Do you know who my mam is?"

Before he could answer, Margaret appeared at the door and in an angry voice said, "Connor, we're leavin now."

Before leaving, Connor leaned into me and said, "Peg, I'm sorry I don't know the answer to that question."

Norah's brooding eyes kept me at bay the rest of the day. She didn't eat during supper and spent most of the evening sulking around the house. Even Dan picked up on her mood and left for the pub after we ate. I wanted to understand what was going on, but knew I couldn't ask her.

In bed that night, instead of thinking about Connor, I replayed what I'd overheard, and still could not make sense of it. Margaret wanted to take me to America, Norah said I could not go, and Hannah was paying for my secondary education. My feelings were conflicted. I was angry that I had been living as one of many in an institution for as long as I could remember, yet I felt grateful that these women cared about me.

CHAPTER ELEVEN

When I returned to the industrial school, the confines of the yard seemed tighter than ever, and the lack of any diversion kept me deep within my thoughts. I'd sit with Patsy against the wall, knitting socks as her chatter loomed around me and a storm brewed inside my head. Anger and resentment toward Norah began to build, and my unanswered questions about who she was stirred a broad range of unforgivable possibilities.

I was grateful when summer's end provided new things to do and think about. Crowded into the rec room with the others, I listened for my number.

". . . number 27, polishing the nuns' dayroom."

As a smile crossed my face, Mary's voice rose from behind me.

"Sounds ta me like ya've become someone's pet!"

I ignored her comment, and took a slight bit of satisfaction when her number was called and she was assigned to the laundry. It wasn't that I hated Mary; I loved her, but her recent actions made me feel that she didn't value our friendship the way I had. There were many days I reached out to her and she didn't respond. I knew she felt abandoned by her sister, and her ego was bruised when she wasn't offered an opportunity to attend Secondary School, but these things weren't my fault.

New bed assignments were issued, and I was placed in dorm two with Patsy and Clare in the first three beds. After moving our things, the three of us walked over to the convent to meet with Mother Bernard regarding the start of the new school year.

"As you know, this is the first time we are sending girls from the industrial school to Scoil Mhuire. I've decided it would be in your best interest to spend as much time as possible with your classmates. Therefore, you will be taking your meals with the boarders and permitted to study in their parlor at the end of the school day. However, you are expected to complete your daily chores each morning before attending class."

Excited by this news, we all thanked her.

"Julia has a uniform for each of you," she continued, "and you'll be responsible for keeping it cleaned and pressed."

Then she dismissed us and I left her office feeling like I'd won the grand prize.

As we walked back to the industrial school, I thought about my good fortune and knew it would be in my best interest to write to Hannah as she'd asked me to in her last letter.

We went straight to the laundry, where Julia handed each of us a small stack of clothing.

"Yer number is inside the collar," said Julia. "Ya can wash and press em in the evenings, after the girls in the laundry are done workin."

I went back to the dorm and laid out my new clothing on the bed. I held the navy pinafore up against my chest, and the hem fell just below my knees. Then I ran my hand over the crisp, long-sleeved, white blouses that featured a rather large scalloped collar. My favorite thing was the thin, light-blue tie that completed the outfit. I folded each piece carefully and put it in the box under my bed. Then I sat down and wrote to Hannah.

August 28, 1949
Dear Auntie Hannah,

Today I received my Secondary School uniform. The jumper is blue, worn over a white blouse with a light-blue neck tie. It is very smart looking, yet fashionable, and I think you would like it.

We start classes tomorrow and I will write to you again soon and let you know all about it. I had a lovely visit to Galway over the summer and met your sister Margaret, her husband, and Connor. They were all very nice, especially Connor. He was quite friendly and encouraged me to consider traveling to America one day.

Did you travel for holiday this summer? I was hoping you'd return to Galway, I had such a wonderful time with you last summer.

I will write again soon.

Godspeed,

Peg

I barely slept that night, thinking about what would happen the next day. I worried about fitting in with the other girls and keeping up with my studies. When morning arrived, Clare, Patsy, and I dressed in our new uniforms and lined up to go to mass. As we walked down the stairs, some of the other girls began to taunt us.

"Look at em in their fancy uniforms!"

"They're Sister Bernard's pets, ya know!"

"Wouldn't ya love ta beat the uniform off em?"

"They may look like boarders, but they're still one of us!"

I hadn't been prepared for the bitter remarks, but I should've known better.

When we arrived at the chapel, Mother Bernard directed the three of us to take seats with the boarders in the pews behind the nuns.

During mass, I turned and looked back at the house children, and some of them stared scornfully at me. One of them was Mary, and I felt as if her eyes pierced me like daggers.

When mass ended, we went to the refectory and sat with the boarders at their table. I quickly chose a chair facing away from the house children. I didn't want to look their way, but most of all, I didn't want to see Mary.

My eyes followed the tray Sister Simone carried and set down on our table. It was laden with freshly baked buns. After we said grace, I took one of the soft, warm buns and savored every bite. She returned with a bowl of boiled eggs and a platter of tomatoes and sausages. I ate heartily, but it was difficult to ignore the presence of the house children behind me eating lumpy, gray porridge.

I was grateful the boarders were friendly during the meal, and glad that nothing was said about us being house children. After breakfast, they returned to their rooms, and we went to do our jobs. On my way to the nuns' day room, I stopped in the kitchen to say hello to Sister Rita.

"Well, look at yerself!" she exclaimed.

"I'm goin ta Secondary School," I said, feeling very proud.

"So I hear. May God bless ya, Peg! Ya look lovely in yer uniform."

"Thank ya, Sister Rita. I'm goin ta stop in and see Erin now."

"Oh Peg, Erin is gone," said Sister Rita. "She got her situation a few days ago. She's workin fer Dr. Dylan's family over in Mount Pleasant."

"That's grand!" I said. "She'll be able ta walk ta town and see her mam."

It would have been nice to be able to say goodbye to Erin, but that's not the way it worked in the industrial school. When it was your time to leave, you were lucky to know about it a few days before, but sometimes you had no notice, and there was rarely anytime for goodbyes.

∞

I could see some of the rooftops in Mount Pleasant from the window in the nuns' day room on the second floor of the convent. I thought about Erin as I quickly dusted and polished the ornate wooden boxes on the mahogany sideboard. She'd been a good friend and I hoped to see her again.

At 8:50 I met Patsy and Clare in the convent foyer, where the boarders had also assembled. Mother Bernard spoke to us briefly about her expectations, and then we left the convent through the front door. We walked down Society Street, passing the dirt lane that the house children used to walk to Primary School. Scoil Mhuire was an elegant building situated just beyond the courthouse. I recognized some of the local girls as we entered the school.

In our classroom, the single pupil desks were lined six rows across and five deep. Patsy sat down in the first seat of the first row, and I took the seat behind her.

Our first class was French, taught by Sister Beatrice, a youthful and energetic nun who spoke with an unusual accent. I thought she was exotic-looking, with her beautiful dark skin and tufts of wiry, black hair sticking out from under her veil. She told us that she was from Corsica, a French-speaking island in the Mediterranean Sea.

She distributed French text books and a red, hard-covered notebook to be used in all our classes. When the lesson was over, she gave us a reading assignment to be completed before we returned the following day. Our next class was Domestic Science, cooking and sewing, taught by Sister Carmel. The morning session ended with Physical Science, taught by Sister Agnes. I'd known her as the cruel nun who pulled towels off of the older girls in the washroom. Sister Agnes was known as the worst nun in Saint Thomas' Convent. She was thin and scrawny with dry, scaly skin, and she never smiled at anyone.

At noon we were dismissed for our midday meal, and I managed to get the same seat I had in the morning. Our meal was a thick, tasty lamb stew with peas and potatoes—it reminded me of Norah's cooking. I tried to pace myself and not eat too fast.

"Yer welcome ta study with us in our parlor after class," said Aileen, one of the boarders.

"Thank you. That'd be grand," said Clare, without any hesitation.

"I'd love ta," said Patsy.

I just smiled and kept eating.

As we made our way back to the school, I whispered to Patsy, "We'd better check with Sister Constance about joining the boarders in their parlor."

"Why? Mother Bernard said we could. I'm goin!" said Patsy. "What else are we goin ta do? I'm not goin inta the yard dressed like this!"

Our afternoon lessons were literature and history, both taught by Sister Theresa. Strands of bright red hair escaped from under her veil and appeared to mar her pure white skin. She also required we read on our own time, and that worried me, as there was no quiet place in the industrial school. So I decided that I had no choice but to join the boarders with Clare and Patsy at the end of the school day.

Their parlor was spacious, clean, and well-furnished. The walls were salmon-colored and a mint green sofa sat between two large windows flanked by heavy, cream-colored drapes. Shelves crowded with books filled one wall, and framed religious paintings hung on the other walls. I sat down at one of the two oval wooden tables in the center of the room.

"Do ya mind if I use yer washroom?" I asked Aileen.

"Sure, it's in the rear of our dormitory," she said, pointing toward a door.

I didn't have to pee—I was just curious. I walked slowly through their dorm with a dozen beds, each covered with a bright white spread and separated by a small wooden chest. I eyed the personal photos and knick-knacks on display. Their washroom had four sinks, each with its own mirror, and four toilet stalls. I picked up a roll of paper in the toilet stall and thought about taking it—I hated the newspaper squares we used.

We studied all afternoon and then ate supper before parting with the boarders. Then we had to endure the discomfort of kneeling through the rosary with the others casting dirty looks toward us, but over time, we learned to ignore them.

Our real challenge arrived in December when the boarders went home for holiday. Patsy, Clare, and I had to fall back into life as house children. Not only did we lose our privileges, but we had to eat porridge and rabbit stew off tin plates, and by this time, I'd come to despise it. Life as a house child now seemed intolerable, and I felt like we didn't belong.

On the Saturday after Christmas, I felt sick as Patsy and I walked together in line to Saint Michael's for confession. The pain in my stomach was so bad, I could barely walk.

"Come on Peg, it's freezin," said Patsy, "Can't ya walk any faster?"

"I've got this stabbin pain in my stomach!"

"Ya better tell Katie or Sister Constance."

"Maybe it's the onset of the monthlies. Ya know—the bleedin that's supposed ta come."

"Maybe it's the food," said Patsy. "We're not used ta it anymore."

The pain continued all weekend, but there was no sign of blood. Monday morning, when we returned to our classes, I could barely walk. It was during our Domestic Science lesson that I doubled over and crashed to the floor.

I woke up in a bed covered with crisp white sheets, looking up at a featureless ceiling. I wondered where I was—it surely wasn't the dorms. I couldn't sit up, so I turned my head to the side and saw nuns wearing white habits running around the large, open room. I was too weak to get their attention and fell back into another deep sleep.

I woke up a second time as a nun in white gently shook my arm.

"I've got to take your temp," she said.

When she removed the glass stick from my mouth I asked her where I was.

"You're in Galway Hospital. You had an emergency appendectomy yesterday."

For three days I lay in the bed dozing in and out of sleep, and the nuns gently washed me and fed me each day. On the fourth day I woke up to see Norah and a doctor standing at my bedside.

"She needs to rest and stay off her feet for about two weeks," said the doctor, and then he was gone.

Norah and one of the nuns dressed me in my school uniform and helped me into a chair with wheels. The nun pushed me to an exit door where a man helped me into the back seat of a black car, and Norah sat beside him in the front giving directions to her house.

The man and Norah took me inside, where Delia was sitting at the kitchen table with Ryan and Rachel. The three of them watched as I was escorted into the back room and put into bed. Ryan and Rachel came to the bedroom door after the man left, but Norah wouldn't allow them into the room. I slept until the evening, when she brought me a bowl of chicken soup. She sat at the edge of the bed and watched me eat. I told her I was unsure of how many days of school I'd missed and was concerned about falling behind in my studies.

"Don't ya worry yerself about that, Peg," she said as she took the empty bowl. "Ya need ta rest."

Over the next few days, Norah brought me my meals in bed and gave me tablets for pain every few hours. The tablets made me feel groggy and I slept the time away. In the evenings after supper she allowed the children in to visit me, but wouldn't let them sit on my bed. On the fifth day she helped me get up, and led me to Dan's chair beside the fire.

"I don't want ya bendin down now and pickin up Rachel, ya'll tear open the incision site," said Norah.

Ryan and Rachel had both grown since the summer and seemed very well-behaved as they cautiously approached me. They sat on the floor beside my chair and I read to them. Shortly after Norah put a kettle on the burner, someone started banging on the front door. She opened it to find a boy who worked at the shoppe down the street.

"Phone call fer Mrs. Hanley," he said. "The party says tis urgent."

Norah looked worried as she threw on her coat and told me to mind the children, but not to get up. A few minutes after she left the kettle began to whistle. Slowly, I took the painful steps across the floor, turned off the burner, and returned to the chair.

When Norah returned, she looked very upset, so I didn't ask her any questions about the phone call. She silently started to prepare supper and I fell asleep in the chair. I was roused from my sleep when I overheard Norah telling Dan about the call.

"That beast of a nun wants Peg on the first train ta Ballinasloe in the mornin. She's worried about her headage count and payment."

"Nothin ya can do, Norah," said Dan. "She's in their care, they're responsible for her."

In the morning Norah and the children walked me to the train station. I was still very weak and had to hold on to the stroller to keep my balance. We walked slowly in the bitter cold winds. I was eager to return to my lessons, but I would have liked to stay on with the Hanleys a few more days. Norah had cared for me in such a loving way that my feelings toward her had softened. I thought about her kind actions, versus my negative assumptions about her. My thoughts were conflicted and my incision was sore, and I couldn't help but weep during the train ride back to Ballinasloe.

I foolishly looked around the empty Ballinasloe depot as if someone should be there to meet me. Then I carefully made my way back to the industrial school, taking small steps and resting periodically. I rang the bell at the blue door and waited, thoroughly exhausted and leaning against the building to hold myself up.

It seemed like a long time had passed before the door opened. It was Sister Constance.

"Peg Joyce, you've some nerve takin off like that!" she said. "How dare you leave the hospital and take a holiday without permission!"

There was nothing I could say, nothing I could do.

"You're picking up airs and graces that you're not entitled to, and I won't have it," she said.

CHAPTER TWELVE

It took several weeks for me to catch up on my studies and physically recover from my surgery. During that time, the boarders were especially kind to me. They carried my books, shared their notes from class, and made sure I was comfortable in their parlor while studying.

To my surprise, even Mary inquired about my surgery after the rosary one evening. I still missed her and hoped we could be close again. Mary had been someone I could confide in, and now we rarely spoke to each other. She'd been the closest thing I had to family, and I thought of her as my sister.

After getting back to normal I took time to reflect on how kind and caring Norah had been to me. She nursed me tenderly and I felt like she truly cared. I couldn't help but feel my growing affection toward Norah and her children. They all treated me so lovingly and I found myself thinking about them more often than ever before. I also wondered if they thought about me. Sometimes I'd imagine sharing holidays with them and visiting Granny out in Moycullen. I desperately wanted to live with them, to share in their joy and sorrow; but most of all, I wanted to feel like I belonged to a family.

In the spring, Sister Carmel gave us civic duty assignments visiting local seniors and sick people on Saturdays after confession. I became fond of one old woman who reminded me of Granny, always giving us tidbits of advice. The visits were welcomed opportunities for us to spend less time in the industrial school, where we felt ostracized by the other girls. Even Sister Constance made sarcastic remarks, referring to us as "the three intelligencia." After making our rounds, all the girls would meet up in Saint Michael's Square and sit and chat a bit before returning to the convent. Maura Glynn, a tall, sturdy farm girl, who had a keen interest in boys, often provided us with a good laugh. She'd sit on the bench, flipping her hair back and waving to the young lads that passed, hoping to get noticed.

"I'm dying ta have my first kiss!" Maura told us one afternoon.

Tara O'Brien, a boarder from Taylor's Hill, said Maura was sure to get in trouble with her obsession about boys.

"It happened ta my sister," said Tara. "She kissed a boy, and before she knew what was happening, he was having his way with her. Sure enough, she got pregnant."

"Did he marry her?" asked Patsy.

"Scoundrel denied it was his," said Tara. "Our parish priest sent my sister away ta have the baby and I haven't seen her since. That was three years ago!"

The boarders shared many secrets, including their hopes for love and marriage and, for some, a career. Through them, I was exposed to a world I'd only glimpsed during my summer holidays in Galway. Although the boarders were more worldly than myself, I realized we were similar in other ways. We shared many of the same feelings and desires as young girls.

I took comfort in learning I wasn't the only one dreaming about going to America. We passed many hours sharing our knowledge of the "American Dream." I felt proud that I could tell them about the first-hand information I had about America from Auntie Hannah and Connor.

My first year of Secondary School had been difficult but interesting, and I became an avid reader. Sister Theresa encouraged my new passion and allowed me to borrow a few books to read over the summer. I'd been grateful to her, as reading would help me pass the long boring days of summer. I decided to bring the books to Galway and read the Shakespeare play *The Merchant of Venice* on the train.

Norah looked well and appeared genuinely happy to see me when I arrived that summer of 1950. I greeted Ryan and Rachel warmly and thought it was sweet when Ryan insisted on holding my hand as we made our way back to the house. While Norah pushed Rachel in the stroller, she asked me about my recovery and how I finished up the school year. I didn't mention the harshness imposed by Sister Constance, but I told her about the compassion offered by the boarders.

At the house, over tea, Norah asked me several questions about my classmates. She was very curious about what towns they came from and their surnames. I gladly shared the information, and added that a few of the girls were hoping to emigrate to America after their studies. She rolled her eyes and then jumped up from the table.

"Oh my, if ya hadn't mentioned America, I'd have forgotten," she said. She took an envelope out of the drawer in the kitchen cupboard and handed it to me.

My heartbeat quickened as I read the return address on the back of the envelope.

Connor Coogan, 87 Fordham Road, Apt. 4B, Bronx, NY

Norah watched as I opened the envelope and removed the letter and four stamps that had been placed in the fold.

June 17, 1950

Dear Peg,

My mam told me about your surgery and I hope you have recovered. I am sure it was painful. A boy from my class was off his feet for three weeks after an appendectomy.

I turn 17 this summer and asked my parents to sign the papers for me to enlist in the Air Force, but they have refused, so I will have to wait another year. They insist that I finish High School and they are still trying to persuade me to go to Fordham College. I hope you had a good school year.

Do you have anything special planned for the summer? I'm taking a job at a local market stocking shelves since we aren't traveling this summer.

I've enclosed some first edition stamps for you to add to your collection. I can send you more if you like.

Please write to me, I'd like to hear from you. I didn't have your address, so I sent the letter c/o Auntie Norah.

Have a great summer and try and stay out of the hospital!

Fondly,

Connor

I showed Norah the stamps and told her what Connor wrote, but I didn't show her the letter. Later in the evening I helped her prepare supper and for the first time Norah talked to me about the industrial school.

"Peg, I know livin with the nuns can't be easy," she said, "but yer doin quite well. Especially now with yer secondary education."

"Yes, I'm grateful for that."

"There's many a child that'd be grateful ta have a roof over their head and food in their belly."

"Yes, I know."

"Ya know, those poor Lowery children, two doors down," said Norah, "their pa comes home with the drink in him every night! What kind of life is that fer them?"

"I wouldn't know," I said in a low voice, thinking to myself that it would be better to live with your family than at Saint Thomas'.

Seemingly bothered by my response, Norah changed the subject.

Ryan slept in a makeshift bed in his parents' room and Rachel slept in the bed with me. She was already sound asleep when I finally went to bed. I looked at her peaceful, happy face and wondered what I was like at her age. I fell asleep feeling sad that I had no memories of a childhood, no stories or photographs.

Norah treated me differently during this visit, more like an adult. She let me make the bread each morning on my own and sent me to town to do errands. I took my time and walked by the Spanish Arches and sat by the pier to watch the boats pull in and unload their daily catch. Once I'd stopped in Saint Nicholas' Church and used the halfpenny Norah gave me to light one of the candles at the foot of the Blessed Virgin Mary statue.

Norah had planned a full day for us at the strand in Salt Hill. I felt like the big sister, holding Rachel's hand in the water while we splashed back and forth with Ryan. Norah even joined us in the playful water fight. We built a sand castle, and took turns filling the pail with water for the moat. It was a perfect summer day and Norah didn't rush us to get home.

During supper, we had a great laugh telling Dan about the grand time we had. He listened as Norah and I shared a banter on who won the water fight and who built the tallest tower on our sand castle. The lighthearted exchange made me forget I was just a guest in their home. I felt at ease and very comfortable sitting around the family dinner table.

Granny came over on Wednesday morning for her usual cup of tea when she was done at the market. She looked well, but repeated herself often. During our conversation she seemed a bit confused and called me Norah. After she left, Norah expressed her concern to me.

"My mam's memory is slippin. Her mind goes back inta time and she talks about the past as if it were taday. The locals at the market must think she's goin mad!"

"It doesn't matter what they think."

"Some days she's fine and other days, I feel as if I'm losing her."

Tears slipped from Norah's eyes. I was touched that she shared the sadness she felt. It was the first intimate conversation we had shared. I reached out and gently patted her on the shoulder, resisting my urge to embrace her. I no longer felt like a child on holiday. I began to feel more like a relative, someone who knew things about the family that weren't discussed outside of the house.

That afternoon we went into town and then to Eyre Square. Norah and I sat on a bench watching Ryan and Rachel play. An older gentleman came over and said hello to us. He smiled at me and then looked at Norah.

"Is this the lass Dan said ya have in ta help out in the house?"

"Tis, Uncle Pat," said Norah. Then she quickly turned to me. "Would ya get the children? Tis time ta go."

I tried to hide the hurt that I'm sure showed on my face. Looking down at the ground, I went to get the children. It sounded like she and Dan told people I was hired help. She didn't even introduce me. I felt deeply hurt by this, especially after sharing such an emotional morning. When I returned to the bench with Ryan and Rachel in tow, the man was gone. Quietly we returned to the house.

In bed that night, I realized I'd been fooling myself for so many years. I'd maintained a hope of being loved by Norah and Dan. Every summer, I'd arrive dreaming I'd be asked to stay. The welcome I felt in their home was not real, at least not the way I wanted it to be. It was like the quote from the play I'd been reading, "All that glitters is not gold." It was just an illusion, my imagination.

My disappointment left me searching for an alternate dream. I began to think more about traveling to America. Receiving the letter from Connor made the idea more enticing. I vowed to myself to end this fantasy of becoming part of the Hanley family. My new dream would be about starting a new life in America.

Over the next few days, Norah and I went on as if nothing happened. It was as if she'd never confided in me or disregarded my feelings in the park. The days passed smoothly, but I still felt the pain.

Delia came to visit on Friday, and Norah invited me to sit with them for tea. I found her inconsistent way of treating me to be confusing. After tea, I excused myself and sat in the green chair by the fireplace to reread *The Merchant of Venice*. Distracted by their conversation in the background, I put the book down. I picked up the top piece of clothing in Norah's mending basket at the chair's side. Norah used a basic hemming stitch that Sister Carmel had taught us. I threaded a needle and finished the mending. Then I started working on the next piece, and kept going until all the clothes were done. When I looked up Delia was gone—I hadn't noticed that she'd left.

Late Saturday morning, I set the table for tea. Norah was expecting her mam to stop in when she was done at the market. She seemed relieved when Granny arrived and cheerfully placed a basket of vegetables on the table. We sat down to tea and listened to Granny talk about who she'd seen at the market and what she'd sold. Norah looked pleased that it appeared to be a good day for her mam in more ways than one. After refilling the teacups, Norah disappeared from the kitchen and returned with Rachel's petticoat.

"Mam, look at these perfect stitches," said Norah, handing the garment to Granny. "Peg took it upon herself ta mend it, and she did a wonderful job!"

I was surprised by this, as Norah hadn't acknowledged that I'd done all her mending yesterday. Granny turned the petticoat inside-out, examining my work and nodding with approval.

She looked at me curiously and asked, "Peg, how old are ya now?"

"Thirteen," I said.

"Are ya still in school?"

"Yes, Granny. I'm in Secondary School."

"Yer lucky ta be in school. There's many a girl yer age workin."

"Yes, I know."

Then she held up the garment, "Ya did this?"

"I did," I said. "Sister Carmel taught us how ta mend in our Domestic Science Class. We're goin ta learn ta cook, too."

"That's what they're teaching ya in school!" exclaimed Granny. "Classes are fer readin, writin, and arithmetic. Everythin else ya can learn here at home, from yer mam."

Norah dropped a dish causing it to shatter on the floor. Then there was dead silence. I looked at Norah. Her face was white, and her lower lip was quivering. Our eyes met for a second and she quickly looked away. I looked over at Granny. Her eyes were darting around the room as if to avoid making contact with anyone, and she nervously twisted Rachel's petticoat in her hands.

I stood up and raised my voice. "Granny, what do you mean—'from my mam'?"

It was more of a demand than a question.

Granny said nothing. I looked over at Norah as she brought up her hands and covered her face. I suddenly recalled that moment seven years ago, when I was taken away from Granny's farm by a strange woman in a strange car. I recalled looking out the back window as it drove away, and seeing Norah hide her face, just as she did in this moment. And then I knew. Norah Hanley was my mam. She'd been there all along, but could not, would not, tell me.

Suddenly, I felt physically ill. An uncontrollable whirlpool of emotions flooded my body. I wanted to charge at Norah and physically hurt her. I wanted to yell and scream at the top of my lungs, but my feet wouldn't move, and a surge of sobs prevented me from forming words.

The front door opened, jolting me out of my shock. I turned and raced toward the door, almost knocking over Ryan as he entered the house. I ran down the hill as fast as I could, a million thoughts racing through my mind.

When I stopped running to catch my breath, I found myself in front of Saint Nicholas' Church. I felt numb and weak. I went inside the church and sat down in a pew. I cried aloud and asked God, "Why did she give me away? How could she give me to the nuns? Why did she keep her other two children and not me?"

I begged God for an explanation over and over again, but none came. An elderly priest appeared at my side and placed his hand on my shoulder and slid into the pew beside me. I felt ashamed to speak to him about my pain. He urged me to have faith in him as a man of God. He listened compassionately as I told him, through my tears and gasps for air.

It felt like I was telling him my confession, even though I did nothing wrong. Afterwards, I looked to him with hope that he could absolve me of my situation.

"Dan and Norah Hanley are fine people," he said.

"But what about me?"

"Young lady, when a sin of that nature occurs," he said, "there really is no other alternative."

"A sin of what nature?" I asked.

"My dear child, it's too difficult to explain to a girl your age," he said. "For now, you must accept your situation and be grateful for what you have."

I paused for a moment, then said, somewhat defiantly, "I'm sorry, Father, but I don't feel grateful right now."

The priest stood up. "It's getting late," he said. "Let's get you back to the Hanleys'."

Reluctantly, I returned to the Hanleys' house with the priest escorting me. I stepped inside behind him when Dan opened the door. Dan and the priest stepped outside and I was left standing there, glaring at Norah. She looked at me with her red-rimmed eyes.

"Peg, please sit down," she said in a barely audible voice. "I'm sorry, I just couldn't tell ya."

I didn't respond—I didn't even want to look at her.

"Please let me explain," she said.

The sound of her voice only angered me, and I couldn't stop myself from lashing out at her. "Explain? What is there ta explain?"

"I didn't have a choice," she began, but then I interrupted her.

"I don't want ta hear it!" I shouted at her angrily.

I meant it. I couldn't listen to her. I didn't want to hear her voice and I wasn't sure I wanted to hear the reason she abandoned me and then lied to me.

Dan came back inside without the priest. It was the first time since I'd known Dan that he looked sullen and tired, and had nothing at all to say.

I left the house and sat out in the yard by the shed. At suppertime, I sat at the table, unable to eat. The silence was only broken by Ryan's comments. When darkness came, I went inside to my bedroom and put on my sleeping gown. I had no more tears to shed, and my pain had turned to anger. I lay down on the bed beside Rachel. She instantly curled up against me. The warmth of her small body was comforting, but inside I still felt pain.

I cried most of the night, pretending to be asleep when I heard Norah come to the door.

The next morning, I stayed in the bedroom until it was time to leave for mass. Then I walked into the kitchen carrying my satchel. Dan and Norah were sitting at the table and a tense silence filled the room, broken only by the children's voices as they played on the floor.

"I'll wait outside," I said and walked out the front door. Dan walked out behind me with Ryan, followed by Norah with Rachel in the stroller. I walked ahead of them, holding my head up and looking straight ahead. Ryan ran up to me and reached for my free hand, which caused me to cry.

During mass I begged God to help me understand. How could Norah have done this to me?

When mass ended, I told Dan I was going to the station. I couldn't return to their house.

"I'm so sorry, Peg," said Dan, in a heartfelt way.

Norah stood behind him, her eyes bloodshot, tears rolling down her cheeks. I felt no pity for her. All I felt was anger and confusion.

"Peg, what about breakfast?" she asked.

"I'm not hungry," I said angrily.

I said goodbye to the children and left for the station without looking back. The train wasn't due for two more hours. I sat on the platform, feeling numb and exhausted from what I'd just been through.

So many questions ran through my mind during the ride back to Ballinasloe. For the first time ever, I wished I didn't know who my mam was. I was not experiencing the joy and love I'd expected I would feel upon learning who my family was.

As I walked back to the industrial school from the Ballinasloe station, I spotted Mary sitting in the Fair Green, talking to a boy. She looked up and saw me coming down the street.

"Hey Peg, do ya want a fag?" she asked, waving a package of Woodbines in the air.

The boy left as I walked toward her. I went over and sat down on the grass beside her.

"Ya look terrible," she said. "What happened?"

Mary sat quietly and listened to my story. When I was done, she leaned over and hugged me, and I cried on her shoulder.

"I always had a feelin there was some kind of connection there," she said.

I composed myself, and we walked back to the industrial school together. I went to the blue door, and Mary jumped the gate.

CHAPTER THIRTEEN

Katie stopped me in the hallway. She didn't seem to notice I'd been crying, and if she did, she didn't mention it.

"After ya put yer things away, the Reverend Mother wants ta see ya," she said.

I ran up to the dorm and unpacked my satchel. At the bottom of the bag I saw Connor's letter. I hesitated, knowing I should go see the Reverend Mother right away, but I decided to reread it again. I was still amazed that he thought about me, and I appreciated his concern about my surgery. I looked at the stamps again and wondered if he already had them or picked them out especially for me. His letter was the only good thing I'd left Galway with. I slipped it into my red purse and put it in my box. Then I rushed out of the dorm, only stopping in the washroom to wipe my face. I wished there were mirrors so I'd be able to see how I looked.

The Reverend Mother was in the foyer of the convent speaking with Sister Constance. I stood off to the side and waited. When they were done, she turned to me.

"Welcome back, Peg," said Mother Bernard. "I hope you had a nice holiday."

I put a false smile on my face and nodded.

"I'd like you to work in the china press for the rest of the summer."

I knew this was a big deal, but I was too upset to get excited.

"Thank you, Mother Bernard."

"There's great responsibility that goes with the job," she said.

"I won't let you down," I replied.

"Report to Sister Rita right after morning mass."

"Yes, Mother Bernard. Thank you very much," I said, trying to show some appreciation.

"You'll take your meals from the convent kitchen," she said.

I felt her eye me from head to toe. I was still wearing my frock from America.

"What a lovely dress," said Mother Bernard.

"Thank you," I said, slightly stunned by her gracious remark.

"Ask Julia to put your number in the collar. I'd hate to see you lose it in the laundry."

"Yes, I'll do that. Thank you."

∞

I found Patsy and Clare knitting by the wall in the yard.

"How was yer holiday?" asked Clare.

"It was okay," I said, preferring not to mention anything about Norah.

"What'd ya do?" asked Patsy.

"Not much," I said and sat down beside them.

In an effort to change the subject, I told them about my new job.

"Are ya kiddin me?" said Clare.

"Nope, she just told me," I said.

"Well, ya can't go ta class if yer workin in the china press," said Patsy.

"She said it's just fer the summer."

While we spoke about my new job, I began to realize just how fortunate I was. So I decided that, for the time at least, I would focus on my life and my future, and try to forget about Norah Hanley.

The next morning Sister Rita gave me instructions on how to serve breakfast to Father Doherty. It seemed simple enough.

"At the back of the china press, ya'll find the dishes. I need one place setting and a large silver tray."

I rushed down the hall and entered the mysterious room tucked under the grand staircase. It was a long, narrow, ell-shaped room. The walls in the rear were lined with glass-paned cabinets displaying a wide assortment of china patterns. I chose a Delft Blue place setting and took ornate silverware out from the deep drawer. Carefully balancing everything on the tray, I returned to the kitchen.

Sister Rita filled the plate with a hearty breakfast. Then she sent me to Saint Andrew's Parlor, where Father Doherty was waiting. He was already seated when I entered the room. I set the tray down and poured his tea.

"Thank you, Peg," he said. I was surprised he knew my name.

I glanced around the room, recalling the last time I was in this parlor. It was the day I was admitted. I remembered eating freshly baked scones with creamy butter and jam. At the time, this room appeared to be so luxurious to me. My thoughts were disrupted by the sound of Father Doherty's voice.

"Excuse me?" I asked.

"That'll be all," he said.

I returned to the kitchen and Sister Rita handed me a fried egg and fresh bun on a plain piece of crockery.

"Take a metal tray from the rack, and pour yerself a cup of tea," she said. "Ya can eat in the china press."

I set my tray down on the counter just inside the door. It felt good to be alone. Unfortunately, I still struggled to dismiss my thoughts about Norah Hanley. Unless I was occupied with a task, my emotions surfaced and my mind raced. I felt abandoned and deceived by Norah. There was no way for me to rationalize what she had done. These feelings were hard for me to ignore.

After breakfast I tried to divert my thoughts and studied the list of bell codes. It was simple—the higher the nun's rank, the fewer strikes to the bell. With only one visitor for Mother Bernard, the day moved very slowly. If I didn't keep busy, I was going to go mad sitting in this tiny room. In an effort to keep myself occupied, I looked through all the cabinets and drawers. One of the other girls had left behind a large tablet of paper and a box of colored pencils. I sat at the counter and drew pictures to pass the idle time.

This new job was boring, except when Mother Bernard sent me into town. I'd take my time walking through Saint Michael's Square and stopping to look in the shoppe windows. Sometimes, I'd sit on a bench for a few minutes, watching the people walk by. Envy raged within me whenever I saw a mother and daughter together. My anger toward Norah grew with every thought of how my life could've been, should've been.

One morning, while I waited in line at the post office, I overheard the woman in front of me ask the clerk about a savings account. This, I thought, would be a way for me to keep my money safe. Leaving anything valuable in the dorm was risky.

During my next trip to town, I opened an account.

The clerk handed me my passbook and grinned. "Savin fer a big trip, are ya?"

"Yes, I am," I said, even though I'd never thought about how I'd spend my money.

"Where would ya be goin?" he asked.

"America!" I replied, without much forethought.

The brief conversation got me thinking. Why not? Why not save my money and go to America?

∞

I made the best of my time in the china press. Each morning, I'd place my purse on the counter next to my box of writing paper, the large tablet of drawing paper, and a book of poems I'd borrowed from Sister Theresa. I wrote a letter to Connor, drew china patterns in the tablet, and memorized poems by Yeats.

I appreciated having this private space—although I spent a lot of time sitting on the stool with my head cradled in my arms and crying. I was lonely and had no one to talk to about the pain I felt. Mary had listened to my story, but she couldn't understand. I even tried to write Norah a letter once, telling her how much I hated her for what she'd done to me. The letter was a mess, and I doubted she really cared how I felt, so I threw it out.

∞

Toward the end of August, most of the nuns left for their beach holiday. Mother Bernard gave me a list of errands to do while she was away. With no one keeping tabs on me, I took advantage of the free-dom. I came and went as I pleased, but kept the list with me, in case I was stopped and questioned.

I took my time and browsed around Cullin's Haberdashery, stop-ping to look at the colorful rolls of fabric. I ran my hand across the cotton weave and wondered what it would be like to wear something so soft. One afternoon as I was leaving the shoppe, I felt a hand land on my shoulder. I jumped and turned around to find the smiling face of my friend Erin.

"Peg!" she exclaimed, and we embraced. It was a rare thing to share such affection with another house child. Her warm hug was comforting.

I missed Erin and our chats in the convent kitchen. She'd always been kind to me, unlike most of the older girls. We arranged to meet the following day at noon.

∞

Erin was waiting at the post office when I arrived. She'd brought two buns for us to eat while we sat on a bench and chatted. She told me about her work at Dr. Dylan's, cleaning and cooking for the family.

"Their home is lovely and I've got my own bedroom," she boasted.

Although it didn't sound appealing to me, I was happy for her. I knew she wanted to stay locally so she could check in on her mother.

Erin was anxious to hear news about the girls at the industrial school.

"I've got ta admit, I miss it a bit," she confessed.

I shrugged my shoulders, "Not much ta tell. It's all the same, just different faces."

Erin's look of disappointment forced me to reflect on the little time I spent with the other house children.

"Well, last night in the washroom I heard that Sister Constance gave one of the new girls quite a whipping. Apparently the girl had a run-in with Mathew Campbell and now she refuses ta go on the milk runs."

"Well, Mathew is quite nervy," said Erin. "I've always been leery of him. I wonder if he's responsible fer Angela O'Neill's condition."

"What condition?" I asked.

"Haven't ya heard? Angela got pregnant! The nuns sent her away ta have the baby," said Erin. "She's in the Tuam Mother Baby Home."

I hadn't even noticed Angela was gone. "Why'd she have ta go ta Tuam?"

"That's where they send ya, if yer not married. Sure, she can't be having an illegitimate baby in the general hospital."

I had no idea a woman's circumstances dictated where she would deliver her baby. Then I recalled Tara mentioning something about her sister in a similar situation.

"Where will she go after the baby is born?" I asked.

"She can't go anywhere. She'll be locked up in there fer at least a year of penance. Then who knows what! Knowin Angela like I do, I bet she'll get sassy with the nuns and they'll send her ta the Magdalene Laundry. And those girls are there fer life!"

"What about the baby?"

"The nuns will sell it ta Americans fer adoption or foster it out till it's old enough ta be sent ta an industrial school."

I was shocked and terribly disturbed by this information. Is this what happened to Norah? Was she sent away to give birth to me? My eyes welled up with tears and I couldn't hold them back. I felt sad and angry at the same time.

"What's the matter?" asked Erin.

"How can Angela give up her baby?" I demanded.

Erin shook her head and looked at me as if I asked a ridiculous question.

"Peg, tis criminal ta have an illegitimate child. Angela can't care fer it. She's got no money, no home. No one would hire her, and even if they did, who's goin ta care fer the baby?"

Tears rolled down my cheeks. I couldn't wipe them away quick enough. I cried for Angela. I cried for her baby. And I cried for myself.

Erin was baffled by my reaction and tried to comfort me.

The words began to spill out between my tears. I told Erin about Norah. I told her how Norah lied to me for years. How I'd visit every summer with hope that Norah would ask me to stay. I told her how the old man thought I was Norah's house help.

Erin rubbed my back and tried to comfort me.

"Believe me Peg, if yer an illegitimate, there's no way she could keep ya!"

"Stop defending her!" I snapped at Erin.

"Ah Peg, she couldn't keep ya. Sure her own family would shun her."

"But I'm her flesh and blood!"

"Peg. Tis amazing that she keeps in contact with ya. Many a woman would deny ya completely!"

❦

I returned to the convent feeling physically ill. My gut tightened and I felt nauseous. I sat in the china press and cried. Now it made sense to me. Sister Rita had told me I was an illegitimate. That's why Norah didn't keep me. I tried to imagine what it had been like for Norah, but I still couldn't find forgiveness for her.

CHAPTER FOURTEEN

$\textcircled{\scriptstyle{6\!\!\!/\,\!o}}$ $\textcircled{\scriptstyle{6\!\!\!/\,\!o}}$

M y encounter with Erin affected me in many ways. Learning about what may have happened to Norah provided me with a reason to ease my anger toward her. Unfortunately, although my mind could grasp that, my heart still had trouble. My feelings toward Norah were still driven by the abandonment and deceit I felt.

I found Erin's firsthand information on life as a housekeeper to be very unappealing. My desire to avoid that lifestyle reinforced the need to earn my Leaving Certificate. I wanted to be eligible for an office position where I could earn money and have freedom.

I knew I had to write to Hannah, regardless of how awkward it felt. So I brought my writing paper to the china press and wrote to her.

August 29, 1950
Dear Auntie Hannah,
　　I hope you and the boys enjoyed your summer.
　　After returning from my annual week in Galway, the Reverend Mother assigned me to a summer position in the china press. The position allows me some free time to read and prepare for the new school year. Classes begin next week

*and I'm excited to return. I've made friends with several class-
mates who board in the convent. Some of them are planning
to go to America after earning their Leaving Certificate. I'm
thinking about that myself. Do you think I might find a good
position in the States?*

*Thank you again for the lovely frocks you sent over. They
fit me perfectly.*

Godspeed,

Peg

Hannah didn't take long to write back.

September 18, 1950
Dear Peg,

*I was so pleased to get your letter. Norah wrote to me
about your visit over the summer. I was sorry to hear about
your exchange with her. Please try to understand that she had
no other option. In Ireland, women live under the rule and
thumb of the Catholic Church and government.*

*I'm not surprised to hear that you, along with some of the
other girls, are interested in coming to America. There has
been a surge of Irish immigrants, mostly young women. The
dollar doesn't come easy, but there are many opportunities to
earn money for those whom are willing to work hard.*

*I wish you the best in the new school year. Enclosed is
some money for you to purchase any essentials you may need
for school. I look forward to hearing from you again.*

Love,

Auntie Hannah

I reread the letter several times, unsure of what to make
of it. She didn't discourage me from going to America, but she

didn't offer any encouragement or assistance either. At least I was remaining on good terms with her, regardless of my relationship with Norah.

∞

The start of my classes left me less time to think about Norah. I studied hard and focused on my lessons. In October, the arrival of the Ballinasloe Fair was a welcome diversion for everyone. During breakfast, house children and boarders alike generated an air of excitement, making plans for their day. The thrill of our anticipation was interrupted by Patsy's sister, Grace, who came running into the refectory that morning.

Her face was bright red as she screamed at the top of her lungs.

"Colleen is up on the fire escape! She's goin ta jump!"

Katie couldn't stop the mob from rushing out of the refectory.

"Don't jump, don't jump!" the girls chanted from the yard, looking upwards.

Colleen was standing on the fire escape handrail, supporting herself with one hand against the building. Her face was visibly bruised and her clothes were torn. She looked as if she'd been attacked.

A familiar voice whispered from behind me, "Sister Constance sent her ta the dairy this mornin."

I turned around—it was Mary.

"Mathew Campbell?" I asked.

Mary nodded her head.

Suddenly, Sister Constance and Katie appeared in the doorway leading to the fire escape. They stepped out and pulled Colleen down off the handrail. We all cheered for her safety. Then Colleen fell to her knees and sobbed hysterically. Instead of helping her up, Sister Constance took the leather strap from her waist and whipped Colleen. I'd witnessed many awful things at the industrial school, but few sickened me as much as this did. I had a good idea of what happened to Colleen, and now she was being punished for it.

That scene stayed in my mind all day. I couldn't enjoy the fair. Instead, I spent the time imaging what Mathew Campbell may have done to her.

Later that evening, after the rosary, I asked Mary if she knew how Colleen was doing.

"They sent her ta Saint Brigid's Asylum," said Mary. "Two men in an ambulance came ta get her. They strapped her down on a board and took her out screamin and cryin."

Secondary School did not offer a class on social justice, but the topic was frequently discussed among a few of the girls while we studied. I began to pay closer attention to their discussions.

"My brothers tell me I'm wasting my time in school."

"Here comes the one with grand notions of a career, they say whenever I come home."

"My sister had ta resign her civil service job once she got married! Her boss said he couldn't keep her on as a married woman, it's the law!"

"I won't marry an Irishman. Sure they think they own ya, like ya've got no rights."

"Why do ya think so many girls are goin ta America?"

The incident with Colleen, the last letter from Auntie Hannah, and my assumption of what happened to Norah all led me to believe these girls were right. Ireland was not a good place for women.

My devotion to my studies helped to pass the time. The Christmas holiday was over as fast as it had arrived. It was the Saturday before we were to return to class when I was summoned to see the Reverend Mother. I walked into her office and immediately noticed the package on her desk. As I sat down across from her, she slid the box toward me and said, "Someone thinks highly of you."

I'd already received a card from Auntie Hannah, so I knew the package had to be from Norah.

I looked at the box; the shipping paper had already been removed, and the envelope on top had been opened. Today more so than ever before, I was angered by the lack of privacy the nuns afforded the house children. They knew more about us than we did ourselves. Surely, they had all been aware Norah Hanley was my mother. Who were they to decide what I should know about? Who were they to hamper my freedom?

I'd always liked Mother Bernard, but in that moment, I felt a real resentment toward her. I felt personally violated that she knew the contents of both the letter and the package.

"Go ahead and open it," she said.

I wasn't willing to give her the satisfaction of witnessing my reaction to Norah's letter. So I put the envelope to the side and lifted the lid of the box. Under a sheet of thin packing paper was a brilliant blue cable knit sweater. My discomfort must have been obvious, because the Reverend Mother stood up.

"I'll give you a few moments," she said before leaving the room.

I took a deep breath and removed the letter from the envelope.

December 22, 1950
Dear Peg,

I hope you are keeping well. Please let me know how the sweater fits. I had a job finding the right color yarn, but Mrs. Maguire at the haberdashery was kind enough to order it for me from Dublin. I was worried I wouldn't have it done by Christmas, as I've got my hands full with the children. It took quite some time to knit, as the cable stitch can be difficult. Granny did the trim work around the collar. The buttons are from a coat Hannah sent me. I've always thought you look lovely in blue.

I've been getting ready for the holiday and have made several plum puddings. Father Kelly from Saint Nicholas' Church says it isn't Christmas without my plum pudding.

I'm hoping Ryan and Rachel don't get sick. Granny is battling the flu herself now. Please put her in your prayers.

We have good news from the States. Margaret, James, and Connor will be coming for a visit in the summer. It'll be nice for you to see them during your holiday stay.

Love,
Mother

"Love, Mother!" I said aloud. "How dare she?"

A fury rose inside of me. All of a sudden Norah Hanley is okay being my mother! Would she say it aloud? Or only write it in a letter? Did she think a sweater was going to fix everything? I balled up the letter in my fist, wanting to toss it in the garbage. Realizing I was in Mother Bernard's office, I threw it in the box with the sweater and slammed the lid on top. I wanted to leave the package right there on the desk, but I didn't want to explain myself to Mother Bernard.

I tossed and turned in bed that night, the box containing the letter and sweater shoved under my bed. No matter how hard I tried, I could not rid Norah Hanley from my mind. A piece of me wanted to be loved by her, to be held by her. Another piece of me wanted to hurt her, to punish her. I couldn't understand how I could have such diametrical feelings toward one person.

Several months passed, and in spite of the cold weather, I resisted the temptation to wear Norah's sweater.

On a Sunday afternoon, a week after Easter, Sister Constance came into the yard looking for me.

"Peg, you have a visitor in Saint Luke's Parlor."

Sister Constance didn't say who it was, and I was afraid to ask. Norah was the only visitor I'd ever had and she was the last person I wanted to see.

I followed Sister Constance into the building and down the hall. She stopped in front of the parlor, but didn't go in. She stood there watching me. I could see Norah and her two children through the glass-paned door. If Sister Constance weren't there, I would have turned and walked away.

"Go on, don't keep them waiting," she said.

I cursed her in my mind as I opened the door.

Dressed in their Sunday clothes, Ryan and Rachel jumped up to greet me. Their excitement forced me to smile and I couldn't help but hug them lovingly. I didn't acknowledge Norah when she came over to me. The children ran over to the window, leaving the two of us alone.

"The Reverend Mother said I can take ya inta town."

"I don't want ta go inta town with you," I snapped back at her.

"Peg, I've travelled all this way with the children. There's some things I want ta talk to ya about."

"What have ya got ta say? Hi Peg, I'm yer mam, but I can't take ya home ta live with me!"

Her face turned white and her eyes began to well with tears.

"Ya can't bear the shame of having me as a daughter, can ya?"

Norah looked at me angrily, "Peg, that's not fair!"

I glared back at her, "Look at where I'm living! I'm like an orphan! That's what's not fair!"

"I want ta be a part of yer life, Peg."

I was losing my patience with her. There was nothing she could say that would make this right.

Ryan and Rachel started running around the room in circles and Norah yelled at them. It was so unlike her, and for a moment I felt the smallest bit of compassion for her. The two of us sat down, emotionally exhausted by the brief exchange.

After a few moments she broke the silence.

"I put a girl up overnight. Her name is Angela. She says she knows ya from here."

My curiosity got the better of me.

"Angela O'Neill?"

Norah nodded.

"Why she'd go to you?"

"She heard about me. I've helped others like her—in her situation and on the run from the Magdalene Laundry."

"Were you in there?"

"No. But I spent a year in the Tuam Home, so I know what it's like."

I was still angry at Norah, but I wanted to know about Angela.

"What about Angela's baby?"

"Died at birth, as many of em do."

I saw a great sadness come over Norah's face. It seemed like a long time before either of us spoke again. It was clear Norah had been a victim of the system, as much as I was. Still, I couldn't find forgiveness for her. Choice or no choice, she abandoned me and then lied to me.

Finally, I broke the silence. "I've got to get back."

I said goodbye to Ryan and Rachel. Norah watched as we exchanged affectionate hugs.

"Wait," said Norah, with resignation. "I've got somethin fer ya."

She took an envelope out of her handbag and handed it to me. "It's from Connor."

"Thank you," I said, taking the envelope. Then I left the parlor without looking back. I didn't want Norah to see the tears rolling down my cheeks. I sat in the lavatory stall and cried for a long time before opening the envelope. It was a Christmas card with three more first edition stamps enclosed.

"Merry Christmas, Peg! I hope to see you in Ireland this summer. Fondly, Connor"

I lay in bed, trying to decide if seeing Connor would be worth a week's stay in Norah's house.

In June the Reverend Mother assigned me to work in the china press for the summer. While running errands, I ran into Erin and told her what Norah said about Angela's baby dying and about her being on the run from the Magdalene Laundry.

Erin nodded her head slowly and pensively, as if she knew something I didn't.

"There's probably someone in the laundry who knows that Norah takes in runaways," she said.

"Wouldn't Norah be in trouble if she was caught hiding one of em?" I asked.

Erin looked surprised that I'd ask the question. "Sure she'd be. The garda would be out lookin fer the runaway. Not many a woman would be seen talkin ta a Maggie, let alone havin one in her house!"

"What a fool Norah is." My statement shocked even myself.

Erin looked stunned. "Fool? I'd say she's a brave woman. It's not right that they lock up those girls. What about the men who put them in that state! They're not condemned fer their sins."

During my walk back to the convent I realized that I was jealous that Norah would risk her reputation on someone she didn't know, like Angela. I admired her and hated her at the same time.

It was a warm day in July and I could see beads of sweat lining the edge of Mother Bernard's habit. She handed me an envelope. "Yer ticket ta Galway. Clare will cover the china press while yer gone."

I hesitated, but knew she was not one I could argue with. She knew I didn't want to go. I turned to leave her office.

"Peg," she said before I went through the door.

"Yes?"

"She's couldn't keep you, but she's still your mam."

CHAPTER FIFTEEN

Katie asked me to mind Siobhan during the trip to Galway. She was a small, shy, eight-year-old girl with stringy, short black hair. I took her brown paper bag and put it with my satchel on the overhead shelf. My patience was short and I didn't feel like chatting, so I told her to take the window seat. I was hoping the passing view would keep her entertained.

Siobhan's presence beside me triggered a memory from my first trip to Galway. I recalled being both scared and excited. I had no idea who I was staying with or why I'd been invited. It was during that first trip that my yearning to belong to a family developed. Each year after that, I felt grateful for the experience, but my desire to belong grew.

Now that I knew that Norah gave birth to me, it changed my perspective. I resented being a visitor. A child's place is with her family, in her home. I should be living in that house, not an institution. Norah should be caring for me, not the nuns. How come I wasn't good enough to live with her? I felt like a second-class citizen. It made me feel unlovable.

I concluded that her annual invitation was made out of guilt. She probably thought it was a way to compensate for what she'd done to me.

I think it was cruel of her to wave family life in my face each year, only to send me back to the industrial school. Each visit caused me to spend many a night praying and wishing to be part of the Hanley family.

With a sigh, I looked at Siobhan and hoped she'd have a better experience. The train slowed down, pulling into the Woodlawn Station, and she stood up. I told her to sit back down and warned her that it was going to be a lengthy journey.

"When you see the Galway Bay, it means we're almost there."

Siobhan's aunt was waiting on the platform when we arrived. I made arrangements with her to meet up for the return trip. While we spoke, I could see Norah holding Rachel back. When Siobhan and her aunt left, Norah released her grip on Rachel, and she raced over to greet me. I was deeply touched by her affection. She was too young to understand we were sisters, but I felt like she loved me anyway. Norah stood aside, twisting a handkerchief in her hand. She smiled and said, "I'm so glad yer here."

I responded with an unenthusiastic, "Hello."

Four-year-old Rachel was quite a chatterbox and provided a pleasant diversion as we made our way to the Hanleys' house. I held her hand and listened as she shared all of the news. She told me that the house was very quiet since Ryan left to spend time on the farm with Granny.

Then she told me just what I'd wanted to hear. "Auntie Margaret, Uncles James, and Connor are visiting."

When we arrived at the house the table was already set. Norah immediately put the kettle on the burner and I went to the bedroom. I put my things away, then sat on the bed, unsure of what to do next. I took a book from my satchel and went out to the yard and sat by the shed.

Norah called to me from the back door, "Peg, the tea is ready."

"I don't want any," I responded without looking up.

One of the boarders, Tara, had lent me *Dubliners* by James Joyce. I flipped through the pages, trying to decide which short story to read first. I chose the story entitled "Eveline." It was difficult for me to concentrate and I reread the first paragraph several times. Finally, I put the book down.

It seemed very wrong that I was a visitor in my own mam's house. How could she pretend all these years that I was just a visiting house child? I dropped my head into my hands. Was she that ashamed of me? Was she that concerned with her own reputation that she could deny me? These questions were only answered by the tears rolling down my cheeks.

I thought about the things I'd heard from Erin and the boarders. They said the local priests and nuns made arrangements for unwed mothers. The mothers were punished and forced to surrender their babies. If not, they'd be shunned by the church and ostracized by the community. My tears turned to sobs. I cried for myself and all the other children like me. I even cried for the mothers. It seemed like a big conspiracy to project all Irish Catholic families as being unblemished by hiding away their illegitimate children. I tried to direct my anger toward the church and society.

Rachel came outside and sat down beside me. She patted me on my back with her tiny hand and said, "Don't cry, Peg."

I did my best to put aside my feelings and pull myself together. There was no good way for me to handle this trip. Being rude wasn't going to help the situation, but it was difficult to pretend I wasn't angry.

⚬⚬⚬

There was little conversation during supper. I did nothing to ease the mood. Dan was unsuccessful in his attempts to engage Norah and me in conversation. When supper was done, he abruptly left for the pub, which appeared to bother Norah. I sat in the green chair with my head in *Dubliners*, pretending not to notice anything. Norah slammed the pots and pans while she washed them. When she was done, she threw the dishtowel on the table and went out to the yard. Rachel became timid in the midst of her mam's anger and squeezed into the chair beside me.

"What's wrong with mam?" she asked.

This situation wasn't my fault. I was the victim and no one wanted to acknowledge that. Oddly enough, I felt somewhat responsible and guilty about the unrest in the household. I put down my book and held Rachel close to me.

I awoke later that night to rumbling in the kitchen. Standing close to the bedroom door, I could hear Norah and Dan arguing. It was difficult to make out what they were saying, but I was sure of one thing Dan had said.

"I won't be walking on eggs in my own house!"

I knew he was referring to the tension between Norah and me. If they sent me back to Ballinasloe early, I'd be facing a severe reprimand from Mother Bernard. I couldn't let that happen, for fear she wouldn't allow me back into Secondary School. Rules about behavior in pubic were extremely strict and the punishment was harsh.

My feelings of anger were re-triggered at the sight of Norah sitting at the breakfast table. I took the kettle from the burner and poured myself a cup of tea. I felt her watching my every move. I knew I needed to change my attitude during this visit, but it was extremely difficult. I sat down at the table and said good morning. In an effort to ease some of the tension I told her about my job in the china press. She sipped her tea and listened intently.

"The Reverend Mother must have great trust in ya. She must recognize how bright ya are. Sure, I'll bet yer the best in yer class!"

I shrugged my shoulders, wondering if Norah was being genuine in her comments. My anger toward her generated a feeling of distrust in everything she said and did.

After we ate, I took my time getting dressed, knowing I'd see Connor. While we waited for the Coogans to arrive, I entertained Rachel, keeping my distance from Norah. I'd be polite toward her, but it was only meant to decrease the tensions imposed on the people around us.

It was nearly noon before there was knock on the door. I greeted Margaret and then James as they entered the house.

"Peg, ya've turned inta quite a young lady since I seen ya last!" Margaret commented.

Connor came in behind them. I hadn't seen him in almost two years. He was more handsome than I remembered. His face brightened as mine paled with nervousness when he greeted me.

We sat around the table eating the impressive spread that Norah had put out. The two sisters monopolized the conversation, catching up on lost time. Connor winked at me and excused himself when he was done.

"Let's go outside," he said.

I followed him into the yard with Rachel trailing behind. She entertained us, putting on a little show. We laughed and clapped while she sang and danced. Eventually, Rachel left us alone to perform for the audience inside the house.

When we were alone, Connor reached over and stroked my hair.

"My mam is right," he said, "You look lovely."

I looked toward the ground. Feeling Connor's touch, and hearing him compliment me, caused me discomfort. It wasn't a bad feeling, but it felt foreign. It was something I'd play over in mind the next few days.

Aside from an occasional appearance by Rachel, Connor and I sat alone outside for the remainder of the afternoon. He told me about his friends at home and his plans for the future. His stories piqued my curiosity about life in America. I asked him what he thought the differences were between the Americans and the Irish.

"I'd say Americans are a bit more open-minded," he said. "Not so focused on religion and customs."

I sat thoughtfully for a moment and then nodded. "The social norms here are awfully rigid."

Spending time with Connor softened my attitude about this holiday.

I sat at the table watching Norah prepare a stew. I wouldn't tell her, but I admired how she cooked with purpose and pride. She glanced over at me and smiled cautiously, not saying a word. I got up and set the table without being asked; it was my way of offering an olive branch. As much as I hated admitting it to myself, I wanted a relationship with Norah. After all, she was my mam. Even though she had lied to me, she'd also shown me great kindness—more so than anyone else in my life.

That evening was a bit more pleasurable for everyone. I could see the relief in Dan's face while we talked about our plans to go to the strand on Thursday with Margaret and Connor. Later, we watched another performance by Rachel, who obviously enjoyed not having to compete with Ryan for center stage.

The following day, I ran errands for Norah in town. It felt good to be out on my own for a while. The breeze from the bay, and smell of the salt water, drew me to the quay. I sat on the pier and watched the currachs bring in their daily catch. It was hard to imagine this body of water flowed into the Atlantic and across to America. So many Irish took the trip across the ocean to find a new life. I hoped to be one of them someday.

Walking through Galway City stirred up many good memories. I knew I had Norah to thank for that. That evening Norah prepared a wonderful meal, exceeding her usual high standard. Dan was delighted.

"Ya've outdone yerself, Norah!" he exclaimed.

Then he looked over at me.

"Ah Peg, sure I know myself, Norah did this fer you, not me."

I smiled weakly in response. I wanted more than a special meal from Norah.

Dan didn't seem to notice the sadness his comment imposed upon me. He asked me if I had plans for work at the end of the school year. His question took me by surprise. I was sure he knew I'd been enrolled in Secondary School.

"I'll only have my Intermediate Cert at the end of the school year. I've got another year ta go fer my Leaving Cert."

Norah and Dan exchanged a look that caused me some concern. It left me wondering if they were hiding something from me. Maybe it was my imagination; I easily became suspicious these days.

I was a bit nervous on Wednesday morning. Granny would be coming for tea when she finished selling her wares at the market. I hadn't seen her since that awful day last year. Norah kept looking out of the window awaiting her arrival. I think she may have been ill at ease about the visit, too. I suspected she was fearful that her mam might reveal more of the truth.

Granny arrived around half past eleven. Ryan was two steps ahead of her. He was his usual boisterous self and I was glad to see him. With a fist full of sour lemon candies, he lured Rachel outside to play with him. I sat down beside Granny while Norah poured the tea. They both acted as if the incident last year had never happened. Like the nuns, they weren't open to talking about anything that made them uncomfortable. Although I wasn't sure I could talk about it myself, their self-interested silence about the situation annoyed me.

I wanted to know why Norah didn't keep me. I wanted to know who my pa was. I wanted to know exactly what the situation was that made her give me to the nuns. I was just getting up the nerve to ask these questions when Rachel came running into the house. She was crying over a scraped knee. Norah quickly got up to comfort her. She washed the scrape and put an ointment on it. I felt cheated, watching her soothe Rachel. My scrapes and bruises went unattended at the industrial school. No one was ever around to soothe me.

It was a long and difficult day for me. I thought about my past—or rather, what could have been, what should have been. I felt angry, abandoned, and unloved. It took great effort for me to keep these feelings inside. The right time to talk about it never presented itself.

∞

That evening, Dan surprised the family with a brand new radio. He set it down on the table beside his chair. Like the others, I was curious about the wooden box with two dials and a meshed screen. Ryan questioned his father about the radio and how it worked. Dan said he couldn't explain how it worked, but promised it would provide great entertainment.

After supper, we gathered around the radio, waiting for the magic to happen. Dan turned one dial and then the other, tuning into a program he'd selected off the listings sheet. We listened to an hour-long situation comedy about the Foley family, the pretend family that laughed over everyday life. I lost myself listening to the show, imagining myself living with the Foley family in radio land.

Friday morning the sun was unusually bright, and there wasn't a single cloud in the sky. It was rare to have a day like this in Ireland. The weather had a great effect on everyone, including myself. Knowing I was going to see Connor also helped my mood. I helped Norah pack the essentials for a day at the strand. We met up at Eyre Square and boarded the bus. Rachel pulled me into the seat beside her. Connor and Ryan sat behind us.

At the beach, Norah and Margaret settled themselves on the blanket, while Ryan and Rachel busied themselves building a sand castle.

Connor was playful, chasing me and then splashing me when we got to the water's edge. The day was more fun than I could have imagined. We walked along the prom and stopped in a shoppe to buy some sugar twists. When we passed a popular ballroom, Connor twirled me around like we were dancing. He made me feel special. It didn't matter to him that other people saw us being silly. I was enchanted by his free-spirited nature. While we sat on a bench admiring the Clare Hills directly across the bay, he reached over and took my hand into his. His hand was large and it felt warm. My palm felt sweaty and I hoped he didn't notice.

"It's a beautiful day!" he said.

"Perfect," I replied.

I acted as if it were my first time seeing the Galway Bay. I was completely enamored by everything he said and did.

In the evening I was tired from the sun and the water, but still excited after being in Connor's company. Spending time with him was worth every bit of discomfort I'd felt during this trip. Norah certainly didn't make me feel wanted, but Connor did.

The house was full on Saturday afternoon. Eight of us fit tightly around the table, enjoying another meal Norah prepared. I sat between Connor and Granny. She took my hand and tucked a shilling into my palm. "Before I forget," she said. I felt a pang of endearment toward her and gave her a gentle hug.

We listened to Margaret share stories about Connor as a young boy. He blushed with embarrassment when she referred to him as "my baby."

"Oh, Margaret! Ya've got ta stop. Look at him, he's no baby boy, sure he's nearly a man!" said Norah.

James interjected, "Ah, she's frettin about him goin inta the Air Force."

"Tis hard ta let go of a child," Granny chimed in.

Connor excused himself from the table.

"Sure, once they're done with their schoolin, ya've gotta let em go," said Norah.

I got up to follow Connor and as I left the room Margaret snapped at Norah.

"Listen ta yerself! It's as if yer not clingin ta Peg!"

I was unsure what to make of that comment. It certainly didn't feel like Norah was clinging to me in any way.

I sat down next to Connor by the shed.

"They're a tough lot in there," he said.

I nodded. We sat quietly, each drawn into our own thoughts. Thoughts about Margaret's comment were quickly wiped away. Instead I thought about the boy sitting beside me. I felt physically drawn toward him. I wanted to touch him, and smell him.

"I'm thinkin about going ta America," I said, breaking the silence. "I'll be done with school another two years."

"You should," he said with a smile that melted my heart.

Sunday was the last day of my trip. I put on my favorite frock, combed my hair and pinched my cheeks to give them color. We were meeting the Coogans at mass.

They were already seated in the church, two pews ahead of us. During communion I made eye contact with Connor when I passed him in the aisle. We exchanged a nod and a smile.

After mass, everyone headed back to the house, Connor and I trailing behind. Margaret helped Norah prepare a big Irish breakfast. I imagined this is what a family celebration would feel like. There was music on the radio, the aroma of bacon in the air, and lots of laughing and conversation. I'd just finished my second cup of tea when Norah pointed to the clock. It was time for me to leave. Reluctantly, I gathered my things from the bedroom.

I went around the table and said goodbye to everyone. Leaving Connor for last.

He rose from his seat and pushed his plate aside. "I'll walk Peg to the station."

My heart pounded with delight. Glancing at the clock, I knew there wasn't much time. I had to meet up with Siobhan and her aunt. We walked so fast, it was difficult to talk. The train was already boarding when we arrived.

"Just in time!" Connor said. I looked around for Siobhan and her aunt. They were nowhere in sight.

Connor handed me my satchel. "I'll bet she's on the train already."

We stood there looking at each other. My responsibility for Siobhan fell to the wayside. Connor had my full attention. I was looking into his eyes. He lifted his hand and took hold of my chin and drew me to him. His soft lips gently pushed into mine and I had my first kiss. I felt an urgency to grab hold of him and pull him closer to me; I resisted. The train whistle blew and I jumped onto the train.

"I'll see ya in America," he said. His face disappeared behind the automatically closing doors. I rushed into the car to look out of a window. He stood on the platform and waved. When I lost sight of him, I brought my hand to my lips, trying to hold on to his kiss for as long as I could. The connection I felt with him left me wanting more.

CHAPTER SIXTEEN

Thankfully, I found Siobhan on the platform in Ballinasloe. I reprimanded her for boarding the train without me.

"I don't want ya ta get a whippin!" I said to scare her. Then I assured her that Sister Constance wouldn't learn about the situation from me. Hopefully, Siobhan's aunt wouldn't notify the convent. I knew if the nuns found out I wasn't with her, it was me that would be in trouble. I gave Siobhan a toffee.

The two of us stood silently in front of the blue door at the convent. Finally, Katie appeared and let us in. The sight of her made me cringe: scraggly hair, rotten teeth, nails bitten to the quick. I walked down the corridor behind her. I could see the oppressive weight she carried.

I put my things away and sat down on the bed. I wanted to cry. Fifty beds, all the same, not a single personal item in view. Angry voices, of frustrated girls fighting in the yard, rose to the open windows. Their sudden silence told me Sister Constance had just made an appearance. I didn't want to go out there.

A few minutes later, Katie was ringing the handbell. I stopped halfway down the staircase and watched the girls rush toward the refectory. Pushing and shoving each other, they looked like a herd of animals dressed in gray farm clothes.

I sat down next to Patsy.

"I'm so glad yer back."

"I'm not," I said, pushing away the tin bowl of rabbit stew. I hated that smell.

"Did ya have a good time?" Patsy asked.

I told her about Connor. She listened politely.

"I miss him already!"

"I don't mean ta burst yer bubble Peg, but he lives in America!"

"Well, I'm goin ta America as soon as I get my Leavin Cert!"

"What makes ya think yer gettin a Leavin Cert?"

I looked at Patsy cross-eyed.

She shrugged her shoulders. "As soon as we turn fifteen, they'll be sendin us out on our situation! Do ya really think they'd keep us here so we could finish school?"

My heart sank. She was right!

At first I felt devastated at the thought of not getting my Leaving Certicate. Then it occurred to me that I'd be out of here sooner than I'd expected. At least I'd have an Intermediate Certificate.

My mind was consumed with thoughts of going to America and being with Connor. My new obsession with him diluted my previous desire to be part of the Hanley family. Of course, that would always be in the back of my mind; but Connor made me feel loved, unlike Norah.

❦

Thankfully, I was back in the china press for the rest of the summer. I'd become less tolerant of the industrial school environment and the other house children. I preferred being alone. Sitting in the small closet, I thought about the things I did with Connor. Sometimes, I'd daydream about a future with him. Other days, I wondered what he was doing and who he was with. There were also those days I wondered if he thought about me, and if he did, what was it he thought. Those were the worst days. I'd feel the deep shame rise within me. No decent person would love a house child.

Fortunately, Mother Bernard still sent me out on errands. Walking through Saint Michael's Square was a pleasant diversion from my own thoughts. I'd look for Erin, hoping to find her so we could sit and chat. She was a happy person, and I'd always leave her company with food for thought. I considered Erin to be quite knowledgeable about life and society. She was someone in "the know."

It was a week before the start of school when we met up at the post office.

"I'll be done in the china press at the end of the week."

"I'll miss seeing ya," said Erin. "Yer so lucky ta be gettin an education."

"I'll only be gettin an Intermediate Cert."

"At least ya won't have ta be a skivvy!"

"I thought ya liked workin fer Dr. Dylan."

"It started out wonderful. Then bit by bit, he started loadin me up with more work. I can barely manage!"

"At least ya get ta see yer mam," I said in an effort to comfort her.

"Sometimes, I get so angry at my brothers fer takin off ta America and leaving me and mam alone."

"Maybe ya'll go ta America one day, too. That's what I want ta do!"

"Tisn't so easy!" Erin said. "Ya need a sponsor in America ta do yer papers and vouch fer ya. Plus ya need big money fer yer fare."

I returned to the convent with a new mission. Instead of dreaming about seeing Connor in America, I'd start working toward getting myself there.

August 30, 1951

Dear Auntie Hannah,

How are you? I hope you enjoyed your summer. I had a lovely holiday in Galway. The Coogans were visiting while I was there and came for tea almost every day. Connor told me about life in America and said he thinks I'd like it there. He told me there's lots of people from Ireland living in New York.

I'm excited to return to school on Monday. I've made some nice friends. Some of them plan on going to America once they earn their certificates.

Most of the girls from the industrial school are sent to clean hospitals in Dublin. Hopefully, with my Intermediate Certificate, I'll get a decent position. This way I can save money and go to America. I understand there is a lot of paperwork involved.

If you have any suggestions please let me know.

Godspeed,

Peg

August 30, 1951

Dear Connor,

I had such a wonderful time with you in Galway. You are so easy to talk to and fun to be with. It was so thoughtful of you to walk me to the station. I want you to know, that meant a lot to me.

All the things you've told me about America make it sound so appealing. I understand that I'd need a sponsor of some sort to go there. Do you know anything about that?

Please write to me at the address on the envelope instead of sending it to Galway. I'm sure you are busy and excited about starting your last year in school.

Tell your parents I said hello.

Fondly,

Peg

PS I wanted to write to you sooner, but I knew you weren't returning home until the end of summer.

That night I felt satisfied when I went to bed. I was putting things in motion to change my life.

On Monday morning, I happily took a seat at the boarders' table in the refectory. The girls shared stories about their summer adventures. Tara got everyone's attention when she announced that she'd kissed a boy. Everyone gasped with delight. I couldn't help it and boasted about the time I'd spent with Connor. They were very impressed that an American boy took an interest in me. For the first time, I didn't feel like I was "less than" around them. Connor boosted my self-esteem in many ways.

The only discomfort I felt about my status, or lack of it, spiked whenever I ran into Mary. Sometimes, I felt like she purposely crossed my path to remind me of who I really was. Making eye contact with her always left me feeling guilty.

This year, our lessons were very rigorous and required additional study time. It was a critical year for me, since I was preparing to take the Intermediate Certificate exam.

Although I was busy with my studies, thoughts about Connor and going to America still loomed. Periodically, I'd check with Sister Xavier to see if I had any mail. Each time, she'd give me a weak smile and say, "Sorry Peg, I haven't seen anything come in for you."

∞

It was a chilly day at the end of October. After dressing in my uniform, with time to spare, I pulled out my clothes box and placed it on the bed. I took the old cards and letters from Connor out of my purse. Patsy came over and sat down beside me while I reread them.

"Ah, Peg, forget about him. Twas a summer thing."

I threw her a dirty look and put them back into my purse.

"What's in there?" Patsy asked. She removed the lid of the box Norah had sent last year and pulled out the sweater.

"This is gorgeous!"

I took it out of her hands and placed it back in the box.

"Why aren't ya wearin it? That'll keep ya warm!"

Patsy was right.

I slipped my arms into the soft navy wool sleeves. It fit me perfectly. During breakfast Tara admired my sweater and asked where I'd gotten it from.

"My mam made it," I said, shocking myself with my own words.

Patsy's jaw dropped and her eyes widened. She was smart enough not to pry and never asked me about it. Erin and Mary were the only two that knew Norah Hanley was my mam.

My disappointment grew with every day that passed without any word from Connor. Feelings of despair and devastation set in. It took great effort to continue with my school work.

It wasn't until mid-December that mail arrived for me. It was a Christmas card from Auntie Hannah. She enclosed a very generous American twenty-dollar bill and a brief note. The note said she was planning a holiday to Ireland during the summer and looked forward to seeing me. I felt discouraged that she didn't offer any help or even acknowledge my mention of going to America.

The Christmas holiday brightened around me, and my mood grew darker. The boarders returned to their homes and I became a house child again.

Four days before Christmas, a package arrived from Norah. It contained a red sweater, drawings of a nativity scene from Ryan and Rachel, and a card that she signed, 'Love, Mother.' Reading those words ignited a feeling of turmoil inside of me again. I wanted to hate her. I wanted to love her. Maybe if I could just understand her. Understand why she did what she did.

After our Christmas breakfast, I found myself sitting with Mary in the back of the rec room. We watched the girls dancing under the garland hung by Sister Angela. She still did her best to make the room festive.

"So this is our last Christmas here," said Mary.

"Thank God," I said.

"When do ya leave?"

"Sometime in June," said Mary. "How about you?"

"August," I said.

"I hope I get sent ta Saint Vincent's Hospital in Dublin. That's where Theresa works," said Mary.

"That'd be nice," I said. "I'd like ta go ta Dublin, too."

"I heard yer goin ta America."

"Who told ya that?"

Mary shrugged her shoulders and smiled.

"Did ya work things out with that woman in Galway?"

I shook my head no.

We sat for a while not speaking a word. I felt the kinship Mary and I shared over the years resurface. I reached for her hand and squeezed it. She returned the squeeze. Uninvited tears surfaced.

"Ya know, Mary, all I ever wanted was ta have a regular family. Live a normal life!"

"It's not in the cards fer us, Peg," said Mary. "We're just house children."

On Friday, January 4, 1952, I received a card from Connor.

December 22, 1951

Dear Peg,

   I'm so sorry I haven't written. My senior year in school has been very busy. I've been working on college applications. The Air Force is still my first choice, but my mam is giving me a real hard time about going. I'm not sure what I'm going to do.

   We've had lots of snow here. My pals and I have earned a nice penny shoveling side-walks. When we're done we go over to the Italian neighborhood and order a few large pizzas. Have you ever had pizza? It's the best! In America, you can find all kinds of people, and all kinds of food.

   I'm enclosing a few more stamps for your collection. I hope you don't already have them.

   Merry Christmas and Happy New Year!

Fondly,

Connor

I dissected each sentence, as if looking for a code. Why was he putting off going into the Air Force? Not to upset his mam? Or in hopes that I'd come to America? I didn't understand why he wrote about the Italians and pizza. Maybe he was trying to say everyone is welcome in America regardless of who you are. Maybe it meant nothing! I was upset he hadn't answered my questions about the sponsorship.

I looked at the stamps in my hand. I felt like a phony. I had no collection, only the few stamps he'd sent me. Connor's letter left me feeling empty. I felt like a fool.

I'd have to find my way to America on my own. Why did I think anyone else would help me?

I listened attentively when my classmates spoke about their plans to go to the States and find good jobs. They all seemed to have a contact of sorts, mostly other family members. The process sounded laborious, requiring lots of documentation. I tried not to be discouraged.

As June approached, I prepared feverishly for my exams. After completing them, I left the classroom feeling confident. Later that day, I bumped into Mary in the hallway. She was carrying the standard brown case given to girls leaving for their situation. I knew it contained a handful of personal effects and one brand-new outfit.

"I was looking fer ya," said Mary. "I'm leaving on the 4:00 train."

"So I see," I said, glancing at the case. "Where are they sendin ya?"

Mary smiled. "Saint Vincent's in Dublin."

"Isn't that where Theresa is?"

"Tis," said Mary.

"Well, if I wind up in Dublin, I'll look ya up."

We exchanged a warm, heartfelt hug. I still loved Mary and always would.

"Peg, I know Dublin ain't America," said Mary, "but I hear it's not so bad."

I nodded and she smiled. Then Mary walked out the door to begin her new life. I went into a toilet stall and cried.

Four weeks passed before the exam results were sent back to the school. Patsy, Clare, and I stared at the manila envelope Mother

Bernard picked up off her desk. She carefully removed three sheets of cream-colored paper.

"Congratulations, girls," she said. "Here are your Intermediate Certificates."

I held it gingerly, trying not to crease it. At the top of the certificate, inscribed in green ink, it read "Intermediate Certificate Awarded to Mary Margaret Joyce." Beneath that, written in black ink, it read, "Proficient in Domestic Science, History, Literature, and French." On the bottom left it was dated June 6, 1952. On the lower right was an embossed seal from "The University College of Dublin."

It was the happiest moment in my life up to that point. Mother Bernard dismissed Patsy and Clare, but asked me to stay behind.

"Peg," she said, "you'll work in the china press until your release in August. You can start when you return from holiday in Galway."

I hesitated for a moment. "Yes, of course. Thank you, Mother Bernard."

She was nowhere in sight, but Norah Hanley managed to dampen my special day.

CHAPTER SEVENTEEN

A lthough I wasn't thrilled about returning to Galway, the idea of having an opportunity to speak with Hannah was enticing. Plus, I looked forward to spending time with Ryan and Rachel. I settled into my seat and resolved to make the best of my holiday.

During the train ride, I wondered where Mother Bernard would send me for my situation. My Intermediate Certificate gave me an edge over the other house children. Surely she wouldn't send me out to be a skivvy.

Norah watched Rachel run over to greet me as I stepped out on to the platform. Rachel appeared to be as thrilled to see me as I was to see her. She was a darling little girl. Thankfully, I was conscious not to impose my resentment on her. My envy of Norah's affection for Rachel was not her fault.

Nothing had changed at the Hanleys' house and the familiarity was somewhat comforting. I guess Norah's life was as routine as mine, except she shared a home with her family and I shared a lonely life with a hundred destitute girls living in an institution run by nuns.

I eyed the new jar of orange marmalade set down beside the butter on the table. That gave me reason to surmise that American visitors had already arrived. Rachel sat beside me.

"Ryan's with Hannah and the boys out in Moycullen," said Norah as she poured the tea.

"Will I see them?"

"They'll all be here on Wednesday after the market."

Then Norah asked me about my exams. I told her I did well.

"Ya've got Hannah ta thank fer that, ya know," she said.

I was surprised by her comment. In the past, for some odd reason, it felt like a secret.

"Do ya know where the nuns will send ya ta work?"

"No. I won't know till it's time fer me ta go. That's the way they do it."

Norah nodded, with a pensive look on her face. I wondered what she was thinking.

After a few moments, she spoke again.

"As soon as yer settled, I'd like ya ta write me."

"I will," I said. I wasn't sure that I would, but it was the right thing to say.

I sensed some mild tension between Norah and Dan during supper. He wasn't his jovial, complimentary self. I was concerned my presence was the reason for his mood. It wasn't my intention to cause a riff in the Hanleys' home. That evening I tried to be as pleasant as possible.

In the morning I made the bread and offered to help Norah with the household chores. She asked me if I'd mind running errands in town. She was pleased when I offered to take Rachel along, but right before I left, she changed her mind and kept Rachel at home. I could only guess why she'd done that. Did Norah fear my influence on the child? Or was she afraid I may divulge her great secret?

I appreciated the space and time away from Norah, although I

felt angered by her decision to keep Rachel home. Norah's control-
ling ways were in clear view for me to see and I didn't like it.

I took my time walking about the town, stopping to look in the
shoppe windows. On my way back to the house, I stopped in Saint
Nicholas' Church to light a candle. Instead of asking God to mend
my relationship with Norah, I prayed that Hannah might offer to
help bring me to America.

The following days were confusing. I enjoyed my time with Rachel.
Her desire for my attention made me feel special. She looked up to
me with admiration, seeking my approval. No one had ever done that
before.

I often caught Norah watching us from afar. Sometimes I felt as if
she enjoyed seeing us together. After all, we were both her daughters.
She rarely left the two of us together out of her sight. I felt as if she
was concerned about the relationship we were developing.

I wondered if Norah viewed me like the Ballinasloe townspeople
did. Was I an outcast in her eyes because I was an illegitimate? That
thought stirred angry feelings inside of me. It was unfair that I had
to carry this stigma because of her sin, while Norah went about life
without the burden. My hostile feelings surfaced during our conver-
sations. I allowed myself to be rude to her, often ignoring her and
leaving the room when she spoke to me. One afternoon, when she
expressed curiosity about where the nuns would send me to work, I
erupted.

"Are ya worried they'll send me ta Galway?" I asked.

I could see my response made her uncomfortable, but she didn't
say anything.

So I provoked her.

"A little too close fer comfort, I imagine."

"Watch yer smart mouth!" she lashed at me.

I left the room. That was the first time she displayed any anger toward me. I knew I was in the midst of a turning point. Going forward, after this visit, any interaction I had with Norah would be dependent on my own efforts. Mother Bernard would not be in charge of me or arranging my holidays once I left the industrial school.

On Wednesday morning, I felt both nervous and excited to see Hannah. I wanted to present myself in a good light to her. I took great effort to tame my hair that morning, flattening it with my hands and pushing it behind my ears.

The anticipation of Hannah's visit appeared to make Norah uneasy. She snapped at Rachel while she fussed in the kitchen.

It was half eleven when Granny came through the front door. Ryan and his two American cousins barreled in behind her. They nearly knocked her over. Then Hannah entered.

"We're here!" she announced.

I'd forgotten what a presence Hannah had. The small figure dressed in white slacks and a floral print blouse dominated the room.

I greeted Granny and the boys first. Then I turned to Hannah. She embraced me warmly. I felt self-conscious when she stepped back and looked me over from head to toe.

"Tis amazing what can happen in a few short years," she said. "Why Peg, you've turned into quite an attractive young lady!"

I smiled shyly. "That's very kind of ya ta say, Auntie Hannah."

The children went outside and I sat at the table with the three women. We sipped our tea and listened to Hannah talk about her good life back in the States. I asked what inspired her to cross the ocean. Before she could answer my question, Norah quickly changed the topic.

"In Margaret's last letter, she said Connor put off goin inta the Air Force."

My ears perked up and I listened with interest.

"She begged and pleaded with him," said Hannah. "I'm sure he'd rather go away than stay home."

"She'd be lost without him," said Norah.

Granny shook her head with disapproval and said, "He's got ta make his own way if he's goin ta become a man."

"How about you, Peg?" asked Hannah.

"Well, I'm not sure where I'll be sent. But my plan is ta save up and eventually go ta America."

"America!" Norah exclaimed. She stood up as if to make a statement. "Sure, Peg, that's no place fer a young girl!"

Angered by her judgement, I snapped back, "Many Irish girls make their way over there!"

"She'd do well," said Hannah. "Sure there's plenty of work fer a bright young girl."

Norah handed me a stack of sliced, buttered bread. "Peg, take this out ta the boys."

Unable to hide my feelings, I leered at her as I took the bread. From the rear door stoop, I heard Norah raise her voice.

"Don't ya encourage her!"

I couldn't believe Norah was trying to manipulate my future. She had no right to try and hold me back.

Hannah appeared at the back door shortly afterwards. She stepped outside and put an arm around my shoulder.

"Peg, I'm sorry. I can't help ya without Norah's consent."

"Why does she have ta consent?"

"A mam has that right," she said in a low voice.

"A mam doesn't have rights over a child she gave away!"

Hannah took me by the arm and walked me to the side of the house, where we couldn't be heard by the children.

"Norah wants what's best fer ya."

"Do ya think givin me away and not acknowledging that I'm her daughter is best?"

Hannah couldn't answer me.

"We've got to get back to Moycullen. Peg, please don't be so hard on Norah. She does love ya, no matter what ya think."

Then Hannah called for the boys and they left.

I returned to the kitchen. Norah was clearing the table. She avoided making eye contact with me.

"I've got this," she said. "Go on outside. Ya've spent no time with Ryan yet."

"I want ta talk ta ya."

"There's nothin ta say."

"But there is. I need Hannah's help ta get ta America."

"There's nothin there fer ya!"

Angrily, I snapped back at her. "There's nothin here fer me!"

"I know what's best fer ya!"

"Oh, is that why ya sent me ta be reared by the nuns?"

"It's not how ya think Peg. I had no choice!"

I glared at her and she continued, "You've no idea what I went through!"

"So I have ta suffer?"

"Suffer? Peg, ya've got a bright future. A good education, better than most young girls I know."

I didn't respond and she continued.

"Yer ready ta take off before ya even see where the nuns are sendin ya! Hannah puts on airs and graces. It isn't like that fer everyone in America. Tis a different world over there!"

I took a deep breath and thought about what she'd just said.

Maybe she was right. Norah's action and words always left me confused.

I felt as if she were dangling a thread of hope before me, and foolishly, I'd try to grab onto it.

The following day Hannah returned with the boys. At Norah's suggestion, we all went into town. The boys ran ahead, the two sisters linked arms, and I took Rachel by the hand. It was at times like this that I felt like part of the family.

At the park, I sat on the bench with Norah and Hannah while the children played. Unlike the people in Ballinasloe, the people in Galway were friendly toward me. Many said hello in passing or stopped to chat a bit about the weather.

On our way home, we stopped at the sweet shoppe. Hannah handed me money.

"Peg, why don't ya go on in with Rachel. It's best we keep the boys out here."

The boys pressed their faces against the window and watched the lady fill a bag with assorted sweets. Behind them, Norah and Hannah conversed with two other women.

As I doled out toffee and licorice to the boys, Norah pulled Rachel to her side. I could overhear her speaking to the women.

"This is my daughter, Rachel," said Norah.

"Oh, she's lovely," one of them replied.

Norah proudly patted Rachel's head while she continued to chat. She didn't introduce me—she didn't even look at me.

I began to feel sick and wanted to cry. As I turned my head away, my eyes met with Hannah's. She was looking right at me. The boys ran ahead, eating their black straps. Rachel held on to her mother's hand as they followed behind them. Hannah came over to me and linked my arm.

"I'm sure the nuns will get ya somethin nice, Peg. Ya've got yer whole life ahead of ya."

"I hope so."

We continued up the hill. Knowing this might be my only chance, I summoned up the nerve.

"Auntie Hannah, I don't want ta stay here. Could ya please sponsor me? It's my only way out of Ireland."

She stopped walking and looked down at the ground.

"I won't be a burden," I said. "I'd find work right away."

She took my two hands into hers and looked at me.

"Peg, it's not that simple. I couldn't do it without Norah's blessin'."

"Please, please, talk to her," I pleaded.

Hannah took a deep breath and then exhaled. "I'll see what I can do."

She embraced me tightly. Her kindness gave me hope. When she released me, I saw Norah watching us with a suspicious eye.

After Hannah and the boys left, the house fell very quiet. Even Ryan settled down.

⌘

I didn't see Hannah and her boys again during my holiday. I wondered if Norah stopped them from visiting.

The few times I tried to discuss my desire to go to America, Norah dismissed the conversation. She'd become stern and abrasive with me.

On Sunday morning she left the children behind with Dan and walked me to the train station. Nothing was said between us and we silently stood on the platform. I knew this could be the last time we were together.

"Ya don't have ta stay. I'm fine on my own."

She hesitated to respond.

"Peg, I don't want ta part like this."

"Then why won't ya let Hannah help me?"

"Peg, I know ya've got grand ideas of goin ta America, but let's see what the nuns have fer ya."

"I know other girls goin ta America! Why can't I go?"

The train pulled into the station. The crowd bustled as people got off and on the train. Norah's eyes welled with tears. I picked up my satchel to board the train and Norah grabbed my arm.

She whispered into my ear, "I don't want ta lose ya, that's why!"

I shook my arm loose and glared at her.

"Lose me? Ya gave me away!"

CHAPTER EIGHTEEN

I looked back and forth between Mother Bernard and the thin folder on her desk. My name was written on the tab. It was Monday, August 11, 1952, my fifteenth birthday, the last day of my sentence to Saint Thomas' Industrial School. I would be released the following day.

"I've arranged for you to work at Kerrigan's News Agent in Dublin," said Mother Bernard. "You'll assist in handling the stock and store front."

I sighed with relief as I digested the information, grateful not to be bound to Ballinasloe, or working as a skivvy for some wealthy person.

Mother Bernard continued, "You'll have room and board with Miss Sarah O'Toole. She's a personal friend of mine."

"Thank you, Mother Bernard," I said with sincere appreciation.

She opened the folder and removed a large brown envelope.

"Here is your train ticket, letters of introduction, and Miss O'Toole's address. I expect to hear from you regularly."

"Yes, Mother Bernard. I'll stay in touch."

"And Peg, I advise you not to share with others about your rearing here, as you'll be poorly judged."

I nodded. I already knew that too well.

She opened her drawer and took out another envelope.

"Please mail this letter. When you return from town, I'll give you a case for your possessions."

"Thank you, Mother Bernard, but I've a satchel of my own."

I left the envelope containing my future in the china press and grabbed my purse. A new feeling of freedom came over me as I ran down Society Street and turned on to Saint Michael's Square. I felt as if the barriers of my life were being lifted.

The post office was empty. I walked right up to the counter and handed the letter and my passbook to the clerk.

"I'd like to post this and close my savings account."

The clerk handed me two ten-pound notes, eight shillings, and fourpence.

"Don't spend it all in one place!" he said.

I quickly returned to the convent, eager to check the departure time of my train to Dublin.

Tucked away in the china press, I held the ticket in my hand. My journey toward a new life would begin at 10 a.m. High hopes brewed within me. Surely, living in Dublin would make me happy.

At five o'clock I heard the nuns shuffle down the hallway toward their dining room. When the noise died down, I went to pick up my meal tray in the convent kitchen. To celebrate my last supper, I transferred my meal onto a Belleek china place setting.

"If they only knew!" I thought to myself as I poured my tea into the delicate cup.

That evening I knelt down in the rec room while the girls recited the rosary in a rote manner. I closed my eyes and prayed aloud with the feelings Father Doyle had instilled in me. There were only a few of us left that could recall his visit.

Surprisingly, I slept well on my last night. The following morning, I slid my hand over the bed sheet to make sure it was dry before folding it. I rolled my blanket and neatly piled my bedding. Sister Constance slowly walked through the dorm doing her inspection.

Wearing a bright yellow frock from America, I stood out in the line as we walked to the chapel. The mass seemed to drag on and I couldn't pay attention. When Father Doherty gave me the communion host, I wondered who'd be serving his meal that morning. I had no idea who replaced me in the china press.

Instead of going to the refectory for breakfast I went upstairs to pack. My satchel was roomy enough to hold my few belongings. I left the gray farm clothes marked 27 in the box under the bed.

From the hallway I looked back and forth into the two dormitories. At least five of those beds had been mine at one time or another.

Katie was coming up the stairs as I went down.

"Do ya know where I can find Sister Constance?" I asked her.

"She's in the refectory," Katie replied without looking at me.

Sister Constance was standing in the doorway leading to the scullery. She watched me walk toward her. I could feel her eyes scan me from head to toe and then settle on my satchel.

"I wish you well, Peg."

"Thank you, Sister Constance."

I handed her a ten-pound note.

Without a word, she slipped the bill into a fold of her long black garment.

Once, I'd overhead Norah say Dan earned nine pounds a week, so I knew it was a sizable offering.

I stopped in the rec room to retrieve my First Holy Communion Medal out of my cubby. Fond memories of Christmas Day and dancing surfaced, but the sad memories followed. Vicious fights between the girls and Brownie's seizure quickly came to mind. I left the rec room and passed through Saint Luke's Parlor to leave the building.

I looked over at the nuns' garden and saw Sister Carmel on her knees. She was weeding around the base of the Virgin Mary statue. I walked over to say goodbye to her.

"God bless you, Peg," she said. "Where are they sending you?"

"I'm goin ta Dublin."

"Well, keep in touch," she said. "We'll want to know how you make out."

"I will. Thank you."

I stopped in the convent kitchen to see to Sister Rita. She had a sandwich all wrapped up for me.

"Tis a long ride ta Dublin," she said, "Ya'll need a bite ta eat."

"Thank you, Sister Rita."

"Now, don't ya forget us!" she said.

"How could I?"

Sister Rita rested her hands on my shoulders and smiled at me. This gesture of affection was the closest thing I'd ever had to a hug in this institution. I held back my tears.

"Godspeed Peg, I know ya'll do well," she said.

Two nuns stood in the convent foyer, so I was reluctant to leave through the main door. Instead, I went down the hallway to the blue service door used by the house children and their visitors. I stepped out onto Society Street holding my satchel and red purse. The tears I'd been holding back trickled down my cheeks. I wasn't sure if I was happy, sad, or scared.

Filled with mixed emotions, I boarded the eastbound train. I sat down beside an elderly woman.

"Where would a young lady like yerself be travelin ta?" she asked.

"I just completed my Intermediate Cert," I said proudly. "I've got a position in Dublin."

She raised her eyebrows, looking impressed.

"Well, yer family must be quite proud!"

I hesitated before responding. "Yes, they are."

"So is it Ballinasloe yer family is from?" she asked.

I thought about Mother Bernard's words of advice.

"No, no. I was visiting a friend. My family is from Galway."

"Sure, I've got family in Galway," she said. "Do ya know Moloney's Sweet Shoppe?"

I felt a surge of panic rise inside me. "No, no, I'm not familiar with it."

The old woman made me nervous. I stood up and reached for my satchel.

"Excuse me," I said. "I've got ta move to the rear of the car, I'm feeling a bit ill."

I took a seat beside a gentleman reading the news. He nodded to me and returned to his paper. I closed my eyes, and tried to nurse my remorse for lying to the old woman. Hopefully, I wouldn't have to do that again.

The train ride was much longer than the one to Galway. I ate my sandwich and watched the passengers get on and off at the many depots along the way. When the train arrived in Dublin, I clutched my satchel nervously and followed the crowd into the Kingsbridge Terminus.

I showed the address of my destination to a garda. He directed me to the queue for bus 145. From the upper level of the bus I looked onto the bustling street. I could never have imagined so many vehicles and people in one place. The city's energy was exciting and frightening at the same time. I got off on the northwest corner of Saint Stephen's Green. I walked along the perimeter of the park and scanned the numbers on the doors across the street.

A two-story brick building with a bright yellow door displayed the number 76, that I was looking for. I pushed the ringer and waited. Miss O'Toole answered the door and welcomed me into her home. She was a petite, well-dressed woman. I couldn't guess her age, but imagined she was quite old. I followed her as she gracefully ascended the stairs to the second floor.

We stepped into an elegantly decorated parlor. I handed her my letter of introduction, which she placed on a small table.

"Let me show you to your room," she said.

"Thank you," I said nervously.

"This is my niece's room," she said as we passed the first door. "And you will be in here," she said, opening the second door. She stepped aside and gestured toward the dresser.

"Why don't you put your things away?"

"Thank you, Miss O'Toole.

I tried to contain my delight at the sight of my new living quarters.

"When you're settled, come out to the parlor."

I stood in the center of the room, absorbing my new environment. The pink walls matched the roses in the carpet that covered most of the wood floor. The bed had a dark wood headboard and a mint-green bedspread. A lace-covered table held a lamp and clock at the bedside. A small oval mirror hung above the dresser against the side wall. I dropped my satchel and pinched myself to be sure this wasn't a dream. I walked over to a small desk tucked into an alcove and sat down.

I gave myself a few minutes to take it all in. Then I put my clothes away, filling one of the four dresser drawers. I placed my rosary beads on the desk and checked my appearance in the mirror before going back into the parlor.

Miss O'Toole was sitting in a rocking chair. I noticed she'd opened my letter of introduction.

"I hope you find the room suitable," she said.

"It's lovely, thank you."

"Let's have a cup of tea," she said.

We went downstairs into her kitchen, where the table had already been set. She laid out her house rules while we had tea and scones.

"Breakfast is served at 8 a.m. and supper is at half six. During the week, I'll give you a bag lunch to take to work. Kerrigan's News Agent is one block over on Leeson Street."

She recommended Marist Church for mass, also on Leeson Street, where her nephew, Father John O'Toole, was the parish priest.

"Carolyn and I attend 9 a.m. mass on Sundays," she said, "You're welcome to join us."

As she spoke, a young girl entered the room.

"This is Carolyn. She attends Loretto College."

Carolyn was petite like her aunt, although she appeared to be quite shy. She said hello and then left the kitchen.

"She keeps to herself," said Miss O'Toole.

When we were done, she gave me a house key and suggested I take a walk before supper to familiarize myself with the area.

I walked the block over to find Kerrigan's. I stood on the opposite side of the street and watched a steady flow of customers go in and out of the shoppe. Then I wandered into Saint Stephen's Green and walked along the meandering paths between the flowerbeds. The park was busy, with children feeding the ducks in the pond, older people sitting on the benches, and groups of students spread out on the lawn. I looked at the fountains and sculptures and stayed within the wrought-iron boundaries of the park. It was a beautiful place and it made me feel safe and surprisingly peaceful in the midst of this big city.

At 6:20 I returned in time for supper. Carolyn was already seated at the table. Miss O'Toole served us boiled sausage, bacon, and potatoes. She engaged me in pleasant conversation about Ireland's history, boasting that Michael Collins, the great Irish revolutionary, was a relative of hers. Carolyn showed no interest in that or any other topic. No questions were asked of me, and I wondered if Miss O'Toole knew where I came from. I left the table well-fed and grateful.

I felt like a rebel that night when I said my rosary while sitting at the desk, but I knelt at my bedside for my nightly prayers. Exhaustion overtook my excitement and put me into a deep sleep.

CHAPTER NINETEEN

Excited and nervous about my first day of work, I kept looking up at the wall clock during breakfast. I clutched my letter of introduction in one hand and lunch bag in the other as I walked to Kerrigan's.

A pretty red-headed girl stood behind the counter completing a sale with a customer.

"Can I help ya?" she asked me.

"I'm here ta see Mr. Kerrigan."

She opened a door behind the counter and called for him. A few moments later, a tall man with tousled hair emerged.

"Ya must be Peg. Come on in."

I followed him into the back room. He quickly reviewed the letter from Mother Bernard.

"Well, ya come highly recommended, so let's put ya ta work."

First, he introduced me to Marion, the girl at the register. Then he brought me into a storage room. I spent the morning unpacking boxes and logging inventory into a ledger.

At half one, Mr. Kerrigan told me to take a break in the room behind the counter. Marion was already in there, eating at the small table. She was very friendly. During our brief time together, she told me what seemed like her whole life story. Then she wanted to know mine.

"So where are ya from?" she asked.

"Galway," I replied.

"Ya came all the way from Galway ta work here?"

Before I could answer, Mr. Kerrigan appeared in the doorway.

"Back ta work, girls."

I was grateful he interrupted our conversation. Talking about myself was difficult. I didn't like to lie, but I couldn't tell anyone I was an illegitimate raised in an industrial school.

Thankfully, Mr. Kerrigan sent me to the storage room and Marion took her position at the counter. We were quite busy for the remainder of the day and had no time to talk.

I left work that evening feeling stressed. I tossed and turned that night trying to anticipate the questions Marion might ask me.

$$\infty$$

I felt nervous when I sat down to eat with Marion the following day.

"So how'd ya wind up working here?" she asked.

"The Reverend Mother in Ballinasloe knows Mr. Kerrigan. She referred me."

I realized I spoke too quickly. I didn't want to mention Ballinasloe at all.

"I thought ya were from Galway."

My heart began to race. "I went ta Secondary School in Ballinasloe."

"My cousin lives in Ballinasloe. Her name is Molly Tobin. Do ya know her?"

The surname Tobin wasn't familiar to me.

"I was only there fer two years. I was a boarder, so I don't know many of the locals."

Marion looked at me and raised her eyebrows. I wasn't sure if she was impressed or if she didn't believe me.

"So, ya come from money?" she asked.

It sounded more like a statement than a question.

"No, I had a scholarship," I said.

Then in an effort to change the subject I asked her, "Marion, do ya have a beau?"

"No, but there's a fine fella I'm interested in," she said.

Then Marion told me all about him.

I realized the best way to handle Marion was to get her talking. Each morning on my way to work, I'd think of questions to ask her.

I spent the rest of the week working in the storage room. From there I could see the customers come and go in the shoppe. Maybe it was because I was on my knees emptying boxes, but I couldn't help but notice everyone's shoes. I hated my shoes. They were standard issue, black, no heel, laces. I no longer had the metal bits on the bottom, but I felt they were clearly institutional.

On Friday, Mr. Kerrigan handed me an envelope with my wages at the end of the day. Proudly tucking my first earnings into my purse, I ran to my room in Miss O'Toole's house. I sat at the desk and separated my money into three piles, room and board, savings, and pocket money.

⚬⚭⚬

During my first Saturday in Dublin, I dared to explore beyond the park. I wanted to be a part of this big city. I walked down Grafton Street admiring the lavish displays in the shoppe windows. Everything appeared to be expensive and beyond my means. I looked with envy at the groups of students going into Bewley's Cafe. All of the people appeared to be full of confidence. I felt self-conscious and fearful of not acting properly. Fearful of not fitting in. Fearful that I was obviously a house child. I looked down at my shoes.

⚬⚭⚬

On Sunday morning I walked to church with Miss O'Toole and her niece. I wore the prettiest dress I owned. It was one Hannah had given me. Carolyn had on a plain dress, but it was obviously of good quality. She also wore a pair of lovely slip-on shoes with heels.

We sat in the second pew in church. The smell of incense, the sound of the organ, and the words of the hymns comforted me during mass. The familiarity gave me a sense of belonging. Even the parishioners seemed less intimidating. I prayed for the strength and courage to survive in this big city.

That afternoon I emptied my dresser drawer and looked over the clothes I owned. I felt grateful for the few nice dresses I had. The two sweaters Norah made for me would be fine for September and October, but I'd need to buy a coat for the winter. My undergarments were terrible, gray from the industrial washings. I had no idea where to buy these items. I surely couldn't afford the shoppes on Grafton Street; they were too intimidating to go into anyway.

I wrote to Mother Bernard and told her everything was fine. I also wrote to Connor and gave him my new address. Unsure of what to say, I decided to wait a bit before sending a letter to Auntie Hannah or Norah. I sat on my bed trying to think of something to do. I wondered what kept Carolyn busy behind the closed door to her room.

In an odd way, I began to miss the house children and the industrial school. I went into the parlor where Miss O'Toole was relaxing in her rocking chair.

"Is Saint Vincent's Hospital nearby?" I asked.

"Why, it's just around the corner on Saint Stephen's East. Why do you ask?"

"I believe a friend of mine is working there," I told her.

I walked over to the hospital and stood outside. Many people went in and came out of the building, but there wasn't one familiar face.

During the next few weeks, things got better. Marion eased up on the personal questions and I began to enjoy our lunches. She asked if I'd like to go shopping with her on Saturday.

We took the bus to O'Connell Street. I noticed the difference in the demographics once we crossed the Liffy River. The people and places didn't appear to be as upscale on this side of the river. Marion took me into Clery's Department Store, where she bought herself a dress. I eyed a section of the store that sold undergarments, but I felt too ashamed to look while Marion was with me.

We walked further up O'Connell Street, looking into the shoppe windows. I stopped in front of Thom McAn. Their window had a large display of lovely shoes.

"Let's go in," said Marion.

Boxes of shoes were piled high against the walls of the store. In the center of the shoppe were a bench and tables displaying a wide variety of shoes. I felt like my world was changing as the salesman fitted me for a pair of slip-on black shoes with a modest heel. I gladly handed over my spending money. I proudly held the box tied with twine containing my new shoes while we waited for the bus.

When I returned to my room, I slipped on my new shoes and danced. Like magic, my self-worth improved. After that day, my stride reflected a bit more confidence.

The following week Marion invited me to see *The Quiet Man*. There were many articles about the film in the magazines we sold. I didn't mention to her that I'd never been to the cinema before. We sat in plush seats and watched the color film projected on a large screen. I felt as if I were being transported into a new world.

Afterwards we met up with two of her girlfriends at Cafolla's for a bite to eat. I had no idea what to order. The girl sitting next to me ordered a mixed grill, so I asked for the same. Visually, I thought I blended in with the group. I began to think life in Dublin could work for me.

It was mid-October when I had my first scare of being found out. I was down on my knees, stocking a lower shelf in the shoppe. A pair of flat, black, laced industrial shoes shuffled past me. I discreetly glanced up. It was Sadie! She was wearing a white smock over a black dress. Still on my knees, I crawled into the next aisle. Sadie purchased a pencil and writing tablet. I watched her leave the shoppe, then overheard Marion talking to the next customer.

"I wonder what she bought that fer," said Marion. "I doubt she can read or write."

"Poor thing," said the customer.

"Must be horrible ta be a skivvy in the hospital," said Marion. "I could never do it."

"Well, she may have no choice," said the customer.

"Probably an orphan or an illegitimate," said Marion. "That's all they're good fer."

I wanted to cry for Sadie. My heart started to race again, and my hands became hot and sweaty. What if Marion found out about me?

When I returned from work, Miss O'Toole handed me an envelope. It was a letter from Mother Bernard.

> *October 2, 1952*
> *Dear Peg,*
>
> *I'm glad to hear you are doing well. By now, I imagine you're all settled.*
>
> *I'd like you to visit Mrs. Bridget McNamara and her daughter Patricia. Their address is 14 Dominick Street. They'll be expecting you on Saturday afternoons.*
>
> *Take the bus to O'Connell Street. Then make your way up to Henry Street and turn onto Moore Street. You should bring something with you—perhaps some fresh fruit.*
>
> *Please give my regards to Miss O'Toole and Mr. Kerrigan.*
>
> *I look forward to hearing from you.*
>
> *Godspeed,*
> *Mother Bernard*

I threw the letter down on my desk, angry that Mother Bernard was telling me what to do. I was no longer in her care. I had my own plans for Saturday. Marion had invited me to watch a hurling match with her.

"We'll meet up with the gang at the field," said Marion on Friday afternoon.

"The gang?"

"Sure—ya can't cheer a team on yer own!" she laughed.

I enjoyed Marion's company, but wasn't comfortable meeting up with more of her friends.

"I meant ta tell ya, I can't make it tomorrow. I've got a family obligation."

"Aw, I wanted ya ta meet my new beau. He's bringing along a few other fellas."

"Maybe next time," I said.

I sat in my room on Saturday rereading Mother Bernard's letter. Despite my feeling of resentment, my dutiful feelings won. Before leaving, I mentioned to Miss O' Toole that I was going to Dominick Street.

"Oh Peg, that's a rough area. Please be careful. Those northern Dubliners will rob you blind. Be sure to head back before it gets dark."

I looked out on the Liffy River as the bus made its way across the bridge. I now thought of the river as the divide of classes in Dublin. I enjoyed walking up O'Connell Street. The thoroughfare was filled with people, cars, and rows of bicycles parked on the meridian. Musicians played their instruments on the street corners. I made my way to Moore Street, which was lined with produce vendors. I bought four apples and asked for directions.

Dominick Street was filthy. Women in black shawls stood in doorways eyeing me. Ragged children wandered around aimlessly.

The rundown buildings weren't numbered. I asked one of the gawk-
ing women which apartment was number 14.

"I'm not sure of da numbers, who's it yer looking fer?" she asked,
in a thick accent, unlike any I'd heard before.

"Mrs. Bridget McNamara," I said.

"Ah, tis Bridie yer looking fer," she said. Her dirty, crooked finger
pointed across the street. "Right over dere, on da second floor."

There were no bells or name plates. I pushed open the door and
went inside. The hallway was dark. It smelled of feces and vermin. I
cautiously walked up the squeaking steps. A man opened one of the
four doors in the narrow hallway.

"What're ya doin here?"

"I'm lookin fer Mrs. McNamara," I said.

He pointed to the first door on my left and then disappeared back
into his apartment. I knocked on the door. There was no response. I
knocked a second time. Footsteps approached the other side of the
door.

"Who's dere?" a woman's voice asked.

"Mother Bernard of the Sisters of Mercy sent me."

The door swung open.

A disheveled-looking woman opened the door.

"Mrs. McNamara?" I asked.

"No, I'm Patty."

"I'm Peg."

"Pleased ta meet ya."

She looked me over from head to toe.

"Well, don't stand dere. C'mon in."

I stepped into the tiny, one-room apartment and handed her the
bag of apples. She took the bag and sat down at a table. I stood there
not knowing what to do.

"Sit down, won't ya," she said, motioning toward the only other
chair.

As I sat down, a frail, old woman watched me from a bed in the corner of the room.

"Hello, dear," said the toothless woman.

I stood up. "Hello, Mrs. McNamara."

"No need fer airs and graces, dear. Sit down. Call me Bridie," she said.

Patty asked me where I lived.

"Saint Stephen's Green!" she exclaimed. "Ah, so yer one of da upper crust!"

"Oh no," I said. "Mother Bernard arranged for me ta board there."

Patty rolled her eyes.

"Where'd ya get that fancy frock?"

"America," I said. "An aunt sent it ta me."

"They say the streets over dere are paved wit gold!"

Patty was funny and the hour visit passed quickly.

"We'll see ya next week," said Patty before closing the door behind me.

I rushed back to O'Connell Street, where I felt safe. I passed Clery's and looked at their display of coats in their window. Maybe next week I can buy one, I thought to myself.

That night I prayed for Patty and Bridie.

On Monday, Marion called in sick. Mr. Kerrigan put me to work at the counter. I enjoyed interacting with the customers, but I was constantly worried one of the house children that worked at the hospital might come in.

One young man lingered after paying for his items. He watched me check out the customers. When the shoppe was empty he came back up to the counter. He introduced himself as Ben, a Trinity College Student. He was well-dressed, wearing a tailored shirt and beige slacks. His presence made me uncomfortable.

"You're quite a lovely girl," he said. "I'd like to take you for pancakes at Bewley's."

I was shocked by his words. They were so unexpected. I didn't know what to say.

"Don't be shy," he said. "I won't bite you."

"I work every day."

"We can go on Sunday."

"I have ta go ta mass."

"How about after mass?"

"No, I can't go, but thank you."

❦

When Marion returned to work the next day I told her about Ben.

"Trinity College, he must be a Protestant," she said. "Lucky ya said no."

❦

I started to recognize there were many different classes of people in this big city. I couldn't figure out which one I fit into.

CHAPTER TWENTY

I spent the following months trying to avoid Ben. He still lingered about the shoppe, trying to persuade me to go out with him. It wasn't only that he might be a Protestant, or out of my social class that deterred me; it was also because I was fearful of socializing with men. It was the same reason I avoided spending more time with Marion and her friends. Connor and I still exchanged letters, but I'd always considered him to be a safe person. He knew about my situation and it didn't bother him. I didn't think people living in America were quick to judge others.

My world in the big city was becoming very small. At work, I'd hide out in the stock room whenever possible. On Saturdays I would visit the McNamaras. On Sundays I attended mass, wrote letters, and took walks around the area. I was desperate for comfortable companionship. I wanted to be around someone who wouldn't judge me if they knew where I was from.

On the last Sunday in November, I strolled along the perimeter of Saint Stephen's Green toward Saint Vincent's Hospital. I was startled to hear a familiar voice call my name.

It was Sadie, who was walking toward me.

"Oh, Peg, it's grand ta see ya!" she said.

"Oh, Sadie, it's wonderful to see you, too."

"Ya look so stylish," she said.

I was wearing the new coat I'd purchased in Clery's.

"Thank you," I replied, feeling very self-conscious and somewhat guilty.

Sadie looked down at her hospital uniform.

"These are my work clothes," she said. "They're very strict at Saint Vincent's."

"Of course," I said. "Sadie, are Mary and Theresa working at Saint Vincent's?"

"Oh yes, there's a lot of us here. We're all workin and livin together. The Mercy nuns provide housing for all of the hospital's domestics behind their convent on Baggot Street. There's about twenty-five of us!"

"Wow, that sounds grand!"

Sadie leaned in toward me and whispered, "We're all house children, but some of the girls are from other counties."

"I'd love ta come fer a visit."

"Ah Peg, the nuns won't have it."

"What a shame," I said, "that's terrible!"

Sadie smiled, as if dismissing my sympathy. "Tisn't that bad. We've got a big open room where we spin records and dance in our free time. It's great fun, and we're all together."

Sadie appeared to be genuinely content with her situation.

"Will ya tell Mary that I'm here in Dublin? I've been keepin an eye out fer her."

"I'll do that."

I left Sadie, feeling oddly envious of her living situation. I yearned for the camaraderie she shared with the other girls.

That evening, Father John joined us for supper to celebrate the first Sunday in Advent. His presence at the table made me nervous at first, but he was friendly and very talkative.

"Did ya hear about the fire this morning on the other side of the Liffey?" he asked Miss O'Toole.

"I did," she said. "I meant ta tell Peg."

"Fire?" I looked up from my plate.

"Yes, on Dominick Street," said Miss O'Toole, "in the tenements."

"One of the residents was burning garbage to warm the place up," said Father John. "They've got no heat. Several buildings burnt to the ground."

"Was anyone hurt?"

"No fatalities," he said.

I was deeply concerned for Patty and Bridie, but I knew I wouldn't have time to check on them until the following Saturday.

Father John interrupted my thoughts.

"Will you be going home for Christmas?" he asked me.

"I'm not sure," I answered, wondering what, if anything, he knew about me.

"You're welcome to celebrate with us," said Miss O'Toole.

"Thank you," I said. Surely, she was aware of my situation.

"Aunt Sheila makes a fine goose," said Father John.

The next morning, I read about the fire in the newspaper at Kerrigan's. It was difficult to figure out if the McNamaras had been affected. The only way to know for sure would be to go to Dominick Street on Saturday.

The weather turned horrific that first week of December. Heavy rain storms pummeled the city. The north of Dublin was hit the worst. Businesses and services were shut down. There was no way for me to check on the McNamaras. No mail was delivered until the following Friday, December 10th. I received two Christmas cards.

December 4, 1952

Dear Peg,

I've been waiting to hear from you. Thankfully Mother Bernard sent me your address in her last letter. She said you're doing well.

Dublin must be very festive during the holidays. I've started a sweater for you, but I don't think it will be finished by Christmas. I'll put it in the post as soon as it's done.

Thank God we've all got our health this winter. Granny eats a raw egg every morning. She said that's what keeps her going. The children are doing well and very excited for the holiday season.

Merry Christmas,

Love, Mother

December 6, 1952

Dear Peg,

I've received information from the Sisters of Charity about the flooding in Dublin. They have arranged for relocation of many of the residents, including the McNamaras. I understand the situation is very bad. I suggest you avoid the area.

I'm sure if you check with the Marist Church they will find a charitable act for you to pass your free time.

I'll be in Dublin for business at the end of January. I'd like
you to meet me at Bewley's Cafe on Grafton Street at noon on
Saturday January 29.
      Please write to your mam. I know she is concerned. Merry
Christmas.

                                                    Godspeed,
                                           Mother Bernard

I wondered for how long they'd been corresponding with each other. My feelings for both of these women were complex. Their acts of kindness through the years seemed loving but also somewhat self-serving and on their own terms.

∞

The following week, I received a Christmas card from Connor. The return address and postage indicated he was still living with his parents in the Bronx.

December 8, 1952
Dear Peg,
      Thank you for your last letter. I'm glad all is well on your
side of the pond.
      I haven't written because I've been so busy with my classes
and college events. The lessons are rigorous, but the parties
and dances make up for it. There are lots of girls, but I haven't
met anyone as pretty as you.
      Fordham is a great school, but I'd prefer to be in the Air
Force. It's always been my dream to fly. Hopefully, one day I'll
enlist.
      I know you said Dublin is grand, but I still think you
would like New York. Maybe you'll make your way over

someday and let me show you a good time. Surely, my mom
and Auntie Hannah would help ya get settled.
  Have a Merry Christmas.

Fondly,

Connor

I didn't like reading about the parties he attended. I wasn't sure
if I felt envy about the socializing he did, or jealousy that he was
meeting girls. Connor's brief and infrequent letters always left me
confused. Was he encouraging me to come to New York to be with
him?

∞

Mr. Kerrigan closed the shoppe at noon on Christmas Eve. He gave
us a little extra in our wages as a holiday gift. Marion grabbed my
arm as we stepped out onto Leeson Street. "Let's go shopping!"

Since it was just the two of us, I agreed.

"The shoppes close at three today," said Marion.

Marion walked swiftly down Grafton Street and turned onto
Wicklow Street. She finally stopped at the end of a long line of people
waiting to get into Butler's Chocolate Cafe.

"I've got ta get a box of these chocolates fer my beau's mam," said
Marion. "I'm desperately trying ta impress her!"

The line moved quickly. Once inside the shoppe, I ogled the
exquisite displays of chocolates in the long glass cases. The rich
aroma was intoxicating. Marion ordered a box of the Christmas
assortment. I did the same, turning over my entire Christmas bonus
to the woman behind the counter.

"Who are ya buying them fer?" Marion asked.

"I'm giving these to Miss O'Toole," I told her—although I hadn't
really thought of that when I made the purchase.

"Why, that's very generous of ya!"

"Well, I can't make it home, so I'll be spending the holiday with her."

I hated myself for lying, but I couldn't tell her the truth.

◌◌◌

That night after Christmas Eve mass, I gave Miss O'Toole the box of chocolates.

"Thank you very much, Peg. I do have a bit of a sweet tooth."

She opened the box and offered me one. I eyed the fancy variety, wishing I'd kept them for myself. The smooth, decadent chocolate melted slowly in my mouth. It was unlike anything I'd ever had before.

◌◌◌

On Christmas Day we attended noon mass and Father John came back with us for supper. After the meal, he returned to the church and Carolyn retreated to her room. I helped Miss O'Toole clean up and then she napped in her rocker. I sat in my room, thinking about Sadie and Mary and all the others living behind the Mercy Convent. I'd have given anything to be with them. I was sure the Hanleys were having a grand time, too.

I went to bed early, trying to end the day as soon as possible. Instead of sleeping, I found myself reminiscing about Christmases at the industrial school. Sister Angela always did her best to turn the rec room into a wonderland. We were so grateful when Sister Constance gave us token gifts donated by the townspeople. Our meal prepared by Sister Virginia was thought to be a feast. We danced and sang as if there wasn't a care in the world. Those girls and the nuns were my real family and I missed them. Feelings of loneliness grew inside of me and the tears welled in my eyes and then trickled down my cheeks.

The New Year arrived and I felt the heavy weight of depression begin to settle on me. Without the McNamaras to visit, I'd become even more lonely. To pass the time, I'd wander over to Baggot Street. Sometimes I'd walk past the Mercy Convent several times, hoping to bump into Mary or Sadie.

I was thrilled the day I saw two girls dressed in hospital uniforms appear from a side alleyway. I ran over toward them and called out to get their attention.

They stopped and turned around. One of the girls was Ellen. When I hugged her tightly, I felt her pulling back.

"Ellen, it's so good ta see ya!"

She smiled but didn't say anything. I felt the two girls eyeing me. I knew it was my clothing they were looking at.

"Did Sadie tell ya I saw her?" I asked.

"She did."

"I'd love ta see Mary. Would ya mind running back inside and askin her ta come out?"

"Mary's gone," said Ellen.

"Gone?"

"Some relation sent fer her and Theresa."

"They went ta America," the other girl chimed in.

"America!"

"Yes, they left on a ship fer Boston last week."

I stood there speechless.

"We better go," said Ellen, "or we'll be late. Bye, Peg."

I stood in front of the convent, unable to move. I wanted to cry, I wanted to scream. I suddenly felt very weak and barely had the strength to walk.

Miss O'Toole jumped from her chair when I entered the room.

"Peg, is something wrong? You don't look well."

I couldn't find the words to explain my grief. She might think I was ungrateful if I said I felt stuck in Dublin. My feelings of envy toward the other house children living together couldn't be explained. I would appear to be churlish if I told her I begrudged my friend's opportunity to go to America and start a new life. I would be ashamed to express the pity I felt for myself. She took me to my room and helped me into bed. Miss O'Toole returned several times during the evening to check on me.

The following morning, I couldn't get up for mass. I slept most of the day. When I was awake, I stared up at the ceiling. Miss O'Toole brought me tea and biscuits. I had no appetite. On Monday, I didn't have the strength to go into Kerrigan's. I felt worse with each passing day.

For two weeks I laid in bed, lonely, sad and depressed. Miss O'Toole nervously popped in and out of my room.

Mother Bernard came to check on me the Saturday I didn't show up to meet her. It was difficult for me to focus on her words as she spoke to me. I felt her cool hand touch my forehead. I tried to speak but instead of words, a river of tears flowed. She sat at my bedside and looked at me with concern.

"Please, Peg, tell me what's ailing you."

"I can't stay here," I replied in a low weak voice.

"I don't understand."

"I don't belong here. I don't fit in."

"Sure you do. You've earned this."

"It's not that I'm ungrateful. It's just I can't be myself. I have ta lie about who I am and where I came from. I feel so ashamed telling ya how unhappy I am."

Mother Bernard didn't respond, but her expression was one of compassion. She helped me out of bed, dressed me, and took me over to Saint Vincent's Hospital. Mother Bernard stayed by my side while a doctor examined me. I was admitted and placed in the emergency ward.

"Peg, you're in good hands here," said Mother Bernard. "The doctor will run some tests. You need to regain your strength. I will check up on you."

"Thank you, Mother Bernard. You've always been so kind to me."

∞

I was prodded and poked for several days. I heard the word "consumption" frequently muttered by the nurses. They tested me for TB and polio. All my results turned out to be inconclusive. I overheard a nurse tell the doctor, "We need the bed, but that nun insists we keep her here." The following day I was diagnosed with a nervous collapse. The doctor prescribed a supervised recuperation. Mother Bernard arranged for me to be transferred to the Linden Convalescent Home in Blackrock, a Dublin suburb.

The Linden Home was run by the Sisters of Charity. I was placed in the women's ward. Most of the patients were recovering from TB. The nuns made hearty meals and brought us to daily mass in their chapel. They tried to encourage us to take walks on the grounds. I had very little appetite and no strength. I spent most of the time in bed, dreading my inevitable return to Dublin.

I thought I was dreaming when I woke up. There was Norah Hanley sitting at my bedside, Dan standing behind her. She was upset, her eyes red, her face pale.

"How'd ya know I was here?" I asked.

"Mother Bernard contacted me."

Norah helped me sit up in the bed and she tried to feed me.

"Ya've gotta eat, Peg, or else ya won't get out of here."

"I don't want ta go back ta Dublin."

"Ya've got a good position there."

"I can't stay in Dublin," I said. "As a matter of fact, I can't stay in Ireland!"

"I don't understand."

"There's nothin here fer me, not even you!"

Norah pulled back. My words jolted her.

"Peg, don't ya think yer overreacting!"

I glared at her. It took all my strength to speak.

"You've no idea what it's like fer me. You've got yer life in Galway. I've got ta hide who I am and where I'm from. I can't be myself without being judged."

Norah reached to rub my arm. She wanted to comfort me, but I pulled back.

"Mother, can't ya see! I live in constant fear of being found out. Of being judged as an illegitimate!"

Norah looked around nervously.

I lowered my voice and continued. "Even in Galway, no one knows who I am. No one knows I'm yer daughter. Do ya have any idea what that feels like fer me?"

Norah began to cry. Dan placed his hands on her shoulders to comfort her. It took a few moments before she could speak.

"Peg, I did the best I could. I tried ta stay in yer life. Ya've no idea the shame I have over this."

"Yer shame is behind ya. Anywhere I go in Ireland, my shame follows me. I am illegitimate. I am a house child. People look down at that."

"I wish things were different."

"But they aren't!"

"Peg, I can't change the past. There is nothing I can do."

"There is something you can do. Help me get to America where they don't even know or care about these things. I can start a new life there."

Norah didn't respond. She looked up at Dan, but he said nothing.

"Mother, if ya really care about me, if ya love me, help me leave Ireland."

I reached for her hand and held it tightly, with all the strength I had.

"Please, Mother, let me go," I begged.

Norah looked up to Dan again. This time he nodded his head and said, "Norah, she's right. Ya've gotta let her go."

Norah slowly turned back toward me until her eyes met mine.

She took hold of my hand and said, "I'll write ta Hannah."

CHAPTER TWENTY-ONE

Three weeks passed and I was still lying in bed at the Linden Home. My health was improving, but my spirit remained low. I'd no visitors since Norah and Dan were here. She'd promised to contact Hannah, but I was beginning to doubt her.

It was just before noon when the nurse handed me an envelope. It was from Norah. I tried not to get my hopes up as I removed the letter.

February 13, 1953
Dear Peg,

It was devastating for me to see you so frail. I hope you've been eating to regain your strength. As promised, I wrote to Hannah. She gladly agrees to do the paperwork for sponsoring your immigration into the US. It appears the process is lengthy; there is much to be done on this end as well. I have enclosed the list she sent.

Mother Bernard suggests you stay with us after your discharge from the Linden Home.

Miss O'Toole has taken in a new boarder and is forwarding your belongings to me.

I know this is what you want and I will do my best to help
you. I hope your expectations are not unrealistic.

Love, Mother

<u>Immigration Requirements:</u>

Passport

Sponsorship Documents

Statement of criminal record from police department

Statement of marital status from Parish Priest

Health clearance from US Embassy Physician

Going to America had been a dream for me. I felt stunned that it was actually about to happen. The combination of excitement and fear of the unknown overwhelmed me. I started to cry and a nurse came over to check on me. It took some time for me to settle down as I digested the news. After regaining my composure, I reread the letter. This time, I took note of Norah's last line, which made me feel somewhat apprehensive. It angered me. Her words caused me to doubt my own desires. I lay in bed reflecting on my intentions. I wanted to live where I wouldn't have to be fearful of being judged. Americans wouldn't judge me. Would they?

Despite the underlying feelings Norah invoked within me, my recovery rate rapidly accelerated.

I arrived in Galway during the first week of March. I was thrilled to see Ryan and Rachel and felt welcomed by them. During the day I helped Norah around the house, and after supper I'd sit with the children and review their school lessons. The first week passed with ease and great comfort. I felt like a normal part of their household, until Sunday evening. Dan had returned from the pub a little late for supper. We were already seated at the table.

"How's yer papers comin along?" he asked me.

I'd been busy settling in and helping Norah. I hadn't done anything.

"Papers take time," Norah interjected.

"Have ya heard from Hannah?" Dan asked.

"We're waiting," said Norah. "It's a process."

Dan turned to me.

"Have ya got yer passport?"

"No, not yet," I responded nervously.

"Well, ya can get the application at the post office," he advised me. "It wouldn't hurt ta get started on yer end."

"Thank you, I'll do that tomorrow."

I wasn't sure if Dan was being helpful or eager for me to leave.

I returned from the post office the following morning ready to fill out my papers. Norah poured a cup of tea and sat down across from me.

"Don't mind Dan," she said. "He can be edgy after he's had a bit of the drink in em. He only means ta help."

"It's okay," I said, wanting to change the subject. I continued to review the instructions.

"It says here that I need ta enclose my birth certificate with the application," I said. "Can I have it?"

There was an awkward silence. I put down my pen and looked at Norah. She stood up and appeared to be flustered.

"Can I have it, please?" I asked again.

"No," she said. "I don't have it."

"Well, what am I goin ta do?"

"I'll get it," she said. "I'll go see the nuns at the Tuam Home."

"I'll go with ya."

"No, no. There's no need fer ya ta see that place," she said adamantly. "I'll need ya ta stay here. I'll go in the morning."

Norah was clearly agitated the rest of the day. She was uncomfortably quiet that evening.

Norah left the house right after Dan the following morning. It wasn't until late afternoon that she returned.

"Here's your cert," she said, handing me an official-looking paper folded in three. Then she rushed about to get supper ready.

I was anxious to see what the document revealed as I unfolded it. It showed my given name, sex, and the date and place of birth. It was stamped with a raised seal. No parents' names were listed. I felt my heart sink. The document validated my feelings. I didn't belong to anyone.

After mass on Sunday, Dan spoke to Father Kelly, who arranged for me to see him the following day.

"Father Kelly will take care of ya," Dan told me with confidence.

When I went to the rectory on Monday afternoon he wasn't there.

"But he left somethin fer ya," said the woman who answered the door.

She gave me a letter of marital status signed by Father Kelly.

Later in the week, Dan brought home a statement from the local garda. It confirmed I wasn't a criminal. I appreciated Dan's help, but questioned his motive.

Hannah's paperwork and my passport arrived during the first week of April. I contacted the American Embassy in Dublin and scheduled an appointment for Friday.

"That's grand!" said Dan, who gave me money for the train fare.

I held tightly onto my envelope of papers during the long ride from Galway to Dublin. I entered the impressive round building in Merrion Square just in time for my noon appointment. The woman at the front desk reviewed my forms and sent me in to see their doctor. "You're as healthy as a horse!" he declared. Then his nurse stamped my paperwork and said, "I wish I was going with you!"

I left the embassy with time to spare. I took a walk and found myself on Baggot Street, standing in front of the Mercy Convent. Two girls in their skivvy garb emerged from behind the building. I smiled and said hello, although I didn't know them. They looked at me curiously. I watched them walk down the street, chatting and laughing, with their arms linked. A well-dressed woman crossed over to the other side of the street as the girls approached her. Her reaction toward them was common, and it fueled my resentment for this Irish society.

I lingered a bit longer, hoping to see Sadie or Ellen, or one of the other girls from Saint Thomas. I wanted to tell them I was leaving Ireland. I wanted to say goodbye.

The night before my departure was bittersweet.

Dan brought home a bunch of bananas and set them on the table.

"Fer old times sake," he said.

During supper Ryan talked about the tragedy of the Titanic, and Dan told him to "pipe down."

My eyes filled with tears when Rachel said she felt sad that I was leaving. I wondered if she'd ever know we were sisters.

Norah remained very quiet.

In the morning Norah came into the bedroom as I packed my bag.

"I've got somethin fer ya," she said and handed me a small box.

Inside was a gold ring.

"It's a Claddagh ring," she said. "Somethin ta remember me by."

I removed it from the box and admired the intricate design—two hands holding a heart, and above the heart, a small crown.

"It means love, loyalty, and friendship," said Norah.

Then she took the ring from my hand and pointed to an inscription inside the band.

"LOVE, MOTHER"

"Thank you, Mam," I said as she handed it back to me.

We sat quietly for a moment.

"Who is he? My pa, who is he?" I asked her.

Norah closed her eyes and smiled. Her face brightened up, as if she were remembering a special moment in time.

"His name is Martin Davin, and he was the most handsome, charmin fella in Moycullen," she said. "And yer the spittin' image of em."

"Is he still in Moycullen?"

"No, Peg. When I told him I was pregnant, he ran off. I think he went ta London, but I can't be sure."

Norah's smile faded and she took my hand in hers.

"Peg, I had no choice. They sent me away ta the Tuam Home."

"Who sent ya? I don't understand."

"My folks and Father Cosgrove. I had no say."

"Why the Tuam Home?"

She turned her head away from me and looked down as she answered the question.

"Twas an old workhouse, much like a prison. There was nearly a hundred of us locked up in there. We were treated terribly. The nuns worked us hard, even when we were in labor. They wanted us ta pay fer our sin."

She paused for a moment and then looked at me.

"Thank God ya survived that place. Many of them babies were stillborn or died while they were infants."

Tears flowed from Norah and I tightened my hold on her hand as she continued.

"I nursed ya fer a whole year. On yer first birthday, they sent me out and wouldn't let me take ya. Twas the worst day of my life."

She pulled her hand from mine to wipe her cheeks.

"I tried ta visit ya, but the nuns wouldn't let me see ya. Then I got the letter that ya were boarded with the Clearys in Lissawullen. I cycled out ta find ya. They were odd people, but they'd let me visit with ya. But when I found ya locked in the barn, I went mad. I took ya back home with me."

"I remember that day," I said calmly.

"Peg, I wanted ta keep ya," she said desperately. "My family couldn't bear the shame. They wouldn't allow it."

"I understand," I said.

"Then Father Cosgrove made the arrangements ta send ya ta Ballinasloe. My mam said it was best. She promised that ya wouldn't be sent ta America fer adoption. Peg, that was the best I could do. Can ya ever fergive me?"

I hugged Norah tightly and whispered through my tears, "I understand, Mam, and I forgive ya."

We held each other and wept.

Little was said during our walk to the bus station.

"Please write," she said.

"I will."

I felt the bond of love when she embraced me.

"Don't open it till yer on the boat," she said, handing me an envelope.

I put it in my purse and boarded the bus. As it pulled out of the station, Norah stood there waving goodbye. She was crying.

The bus was crowded; many of the other passengers were also going to the port. I looked at my ring and momentarily questioned my departure. My strength came from deep inside; I knew I didn't belong here.

My excitement grew when shouts of joy came from the other passengers. Through the bus window, I admired the stately ship in the harbor. When the bus stopped, people pushed and shoved each other. Everyone was eager to get off the bus and onto the ship.

Along with the others, I queued up at the terminal. A handsome young man dressed in a uniform looked over my papers and passport. He reminded me of Connor.

"I hate ta see a pretty lass like yerself leave Ireland. Look me up if ya ever come back!"

I smiled, but didn't answer him. I really didn't know if I'd ever want to come back.

I stood on the deck of the S.S. America, looking at the shoreline. The ship's horn blew as it began to pull out of the harbor. I removed the envelope from my purse. It held a photograph of a young woman holding a small girl. I recalled the day it was taken; it was just before I had left Moycullen for Ballinasloe. Tears welled up in my eyes, but I felt surprisingly calm as we sailed toward the wide-open Atlantic Ocean.

Discussion Questions

1. Should Norah have fought with her parents to keep her daughter?

2. Why do you think Sister Constance believed it was in the best interest of the children to treat them all the same? Do you think she had any affectionate feelings for the children?

3. Do you think it was the town's residents or the Sisters of Mercy that preferred to separate the house children and the town's children?

4. Do you think the house children felt family bonds among themselves?

5. Was it a loving act or unfair of Norah to stay in Peg's life?

6. Was Peg's exposure to the Hanley family a benefit or a hindrance?

7. What was the source of Peg's strength to grow as a person?

8. Why do you think the boarders were so accepting of Peg, Patsy, and Clare?

9. Why do you think Mother Bernard kept tabs on Peg after she left Saint Thomas?

10. Why do you think Dan encouraged Norah to sign off on Peg's emigration?

11. Do you think Peg forgave Norah?

12. Given the choice, do you think Peg would have stayed in Ireland if she could have lived with the Hanley family?

Acknowledgments

I am sincerely grateful to my family and friends who have supported me throughout the long process of researching and writing *The House Children.*

A very special thank you to three people who were pivotal in my journey. Mitchell Resk, my son, who gave me books on how to write a book, hoping they would encourage me to write the story I had talked about for so long. Benee Knauer, my editor, who tactfully guided me through the process of "fleshing it out." Working with her has been a priceless education. Last but not least, Frank Daniele, my husband, whose love and unyielding support gave me the strength and confidence to navigate the complex road to publication.

About the Author

© Naomi Maxwell

Heidi Daniele's passion for history and genealogy opened the door for her debut novel, *The House Children*. An empty nester, living in the Hudson Valley with her husband, Heidi enjoys gardening, photography, and exploring her family tree. She has a degree in Communications and Media Arts and has worked on several short independent films. She earned the Learning in Progress Award for Excellence at a Dutchess Community College Film Festival for coproducing, writing, directing, filming, and editing the film, *Final Decisions*.

Volunteer work: The Lisa Libraries—The Lisa Libraries donates new children's books and small libraries to organizations that work with kids in poor and under-served areas.

SELECTED TITLES FROM SPARKPRESS

SparkPress is an independent boutique publisher delivering high-quality, entertaining, and engaging content that enhances readers' lives, with a special focus on female-driven work.
Visit us at www.gosparkpress.com

The Leaving Year, Pam McGaffin, $16.95, 9781943006816
As the Summer of Love comes to an end, 15-year-old Ida Petrovich waits for a father who never comes home. While commercial fishing in Alaska, he is lost at sea, but with no body and no wreckage, Ida and her mother are forced to accept a "presumed" death that tests their already strained relationship. While still in shock over the loss of her father, Ida overhears an adult conversation that shatters everything she thought she knew about him. This prompts her to set out on a search for the truth that takes her from her Washington State hometown to Southeast Alaska.

Bear Witness, Melissa Clark. $15, 978-1-94071-675-6
What if you witnessed the kidnapping of your best friend? This is when life changed for twelve-year-old Paige Bellen. This book explores the aftermath of a crime in a small community, and what it means when tragedy colors the experience of being a young adult.

But Not Forever, Jan Von Schleh, $16.95, 978-1-943006-58-8
When identical fifteen-year-old girls are mysteriously switched in time, they discover the love that's been missing in their lives. Torn, both want to go home, but neither wants to give up what they now have.

The Rules of Half, Jenna Patrick, $16.95, 978-1-943006-18-2
When an orphaned teen claims he's her biological father, Will Fletcher—a manic-depressant who's sworn to never be a parent again—must come to terms with his illness and his tragic past if he is to save her from the streets. This explores what it is to be an atypical family in a small town and to be mentally ill in the wake of a tragedy.

ABOUT SPARKPRESS

SparkPress is an independent, hybrid imprint focused on merging the best of the traditional publishing model with new and innovative strategies. We deliver high-quality, entertaining, and engaging content that enhances readers' lives. We are proud to bring to market a list of *New York Times* best-selling, award-winning, and debut authors who represent a wide array of genres, as well as our established, industry-wide reputation for creative, results-driven success in working with authors. SparkPress, a BookSparks imprint, is a division of SparkPoint Studio LLC.

Learn more at GoSparkPress.com